who saw a few
pages go through
his computer.

Many Thanks,

Bob Metcalfe

THE SAIGON WIFE

Robert Metcalfe

MINERVA PRESS
MONTREUX   LONDON   WASHINGTON

THE SAIGON WIFE
Copyright © Robert Metcalfe 1996

All Rights Reserved

ISBN 1 85863 998 0

First Published 1996 by
MINERVA PRESS
195 Knightsbridge
London SW7 1RE

Printed in Great Britain by
B.W.D. Ltd, Northolt, Middlesex

THE SAIGON WIFE

Foreword

In 1964, American help for South Vietnam's war against Viet Cong insurgents was confined to money, arms, military advisers and trainers. But that was about to change, and so were many lives that were touched by the war, directly or indirectly.

On August 2, in what became known as 'the Tonkin Gulf incident', North Vietnam patrol boats attacked the US destroyer 'Maddox' as it carried out electronic eavesdropping on Hanoi. In a 20-minute skirmish, one bullet hit the 'Maddox'. Two days later, the 'Maddox' and the destroyer 'Turner Joy' reported that they had fought off more patrol-boat attacks in the Gulf. Neither destroyer was hit, and there was never any hard evidence that the attacks took place.

But an angry President Lyndon Johnson, armed with a congressional resolution that allowed him to conduct the Vietnam adventure pretty well as he wished, retaliated by sending the first American air strikes against North Vietnam: 64 sorties of bombers hammered northern ports, destroying or damaging 25 vessels.

North Vietnam struck back, slipping thousands of troops into the South to help the Viet Cong; in the next year, the insurgents attacked villages, blew up bridges, mined roads, and murdered more than 4,000 village and provincial leaders.

Johnson again raised the stakes: he sent the South more and more military aid and, finally, troops. The first marines landed at Danang on March 8, 1965 (two years later there were half a million American troops in Vietnam), and to clear the field for an all-out war, Johnson ordered US government employees, military and civilian, to get their wives and children out of the country.

Some families went to US bases in the Pacific or home to the States. But many moved to Bangkok: the Thai capital was only an hour or so by air from Saigon so husbands and fathers could easily visit now and then. And Thailand had a large American presence: an

v

extensive diplomatic mission, aid agencies, the Peace Corps, radio's Voice of America, the US Information Service, scores of military advisers and trainers, troops in a regional defence alliance, and the US Air Force which attacked North Vietnam from bases in the North-East.

In Bangkok, hundreds of American dependants lived comfortably in rented houses or apartments. They had servants for a few dollars a month, American and other English-language schools for their children, American enclaves with swimming pools, tennis courts and cinemas, American doctors, teachers, bankers, lawyers, ministers and merchants, and American food, liquor, cigarettes, appliances and many other amenities of home available at one of those grand US military super stores, the Post Exchange, or the 'PX' as it was simply called.

The families from Vietnam fitted in quite naturally with the established Americans, but the wives soon acquired an identity of their own: they became known in Bangkok as 'the Saigon wives'.

One was a woman called Madli. 'The Saigon Wife' is about Madli, her husband and their two children, and these particular few of her many Bangkok friends and playmates:

WILMA - like Madli, a Saigon wife whose husband is with the American Embassy in Saigon; a refined and attractive Bostonian of 48; bobbed black hair, humorous blue eyes, and a full and well-preserved figure.

JILL - a Jamaican mulatto of 37, striking looks and a sensual and fiery nature; an artist and fashion designer.

BETTY - a shapely, pretty Londoner of 26; warm brown eyes and disposition, and long, lustrous auburn hair; she is with the English-language 'Siam World'.

SUSAN - a Canadian, of Betty's age, a blue-eyed blonde with plain but pleasant looks; teaches English at the Royal Thai Military Academy for US military advisers.

MARIA - a slim, dark-eyed, raven-haired beauty of 23, only daughter of a Greek shipping family in Bangkok.

JIM - a mid-west American, 33, blond good looks, average height, and a spare, muscular build; sells liquor and tobacco products to the PX and US servicemen clubs and canteens.

CARL - a big, burly, green-eyed, ginger-haired Yank of 46; a pilot with Unistates Air, a maverick airline on mysterious missions in Southeast Asia.

FRANK - a US Air Force major; 38, tall and husky, has black crew-cut, black eyes, and the hawkish features of an American Indian.

WARD - English, about 40, grey eyes, short brown hair, fine good looks and a fairly tall, athletic build; a military planning officer at Seato, a Southeast Asia defence alliance.

FREDDY - an Australian of 36, medium height, rather thin, brown eyes, wavy black hair and slightly prominent teeth; a press officer at Seato's Bangkok headquarters.

BEATRICE AND THE REVEREND RALPH - New Zealand Anglican missionaries in their late fifties; she's short, plump and motherly; he's a head taller, flabby, awkward and pale-eyed.

CAPTAIN SOMSAK - short, slight, dark and fortyish; has fluent English and a quick and disarming smile; heads the foreign section of Bangkok's Metropolitan Police Division.

Now turn the page and see what awaits them in *The Saigon Wife*.

Chapter One

Madli went to her grave in a cocktail dress. It suited the journey: she used to joke that the endless receptions and parties among the many foreign residents of Bangkok would be the death of her. And they might just as well have had something to do with her sudden passing, for all that came of the hours of morbid speculation by the few friends and lovers who now gathered with her husband and children in the old Anglican church on Convent Lane to see her off.

The dress was all she wore. It was a simple, elegant mini frock in white Thai silk that shaped her full hips, prominent nipples and *mons veneris*, and left much of her golden body enticingly bare against the red-velvet lining of her teak casket: slender feet and legs, graceful arms, neck and shoulders, and generous portions of her firm breasts which had been reinforced by plastic surgery on her trip to Tokyo after she turned forty last summer.

She looked years younger. Fair and flawless skin moulded a lofty brow, high cheekbones and a delicate nose and chin; and the long yellow hair brushed over the scarlet pillow might have been a schoolgirl's. Her only make-up was a light mascara on the delicate lashes that curled from rather deep and dramatic lids, her only jewellery a tiny silver cross on a thin silver chain between her breasts.

Madli's casket lay on a low table in the centre of the small church, and her beauty was brushed by light from an open doorway on the shade side. She looked expectant, as if eager to open her compelling blue eyes and soft lips and abandon her lovely body once more to fiery passion - a transformation due to the cosmetic skills of the Chinese undertaker. For on the previous morning, lying naked on her wide bed, Madli's features had been twisted in terrible agony or fear, her pink silk sheets drenched in the blood from a bullet hole in her left breast.

Somsak turned away from Madli's appealing corpse. She had disturbed him in life, and now in death, but he was distracted by a sudden whine in the Reverend Ralph's doleful recital of the funeral service at the head of the casket. His substantial back, Somsak noticed, had intercepted a scorching shaft of tropical sun that pierced the derelict wooden shutters on the other side of the decaying church, and sweat dripped from his pallid jowls onto the open prayer book he held against his dark blue blazer.

Tiptoeing to her husband's side, Beatrice produced a large red bandanna from her voluminous green-cotton dress and began mopping his soggy face. And now, his delivery fitfully muffled by sweeps of the bandanna, he intoned something about the certainty of Madli's everlasting life in the kingdom of heaven.

But Somsak, a devout Buddhist, was equally certain of Madli's rebirth to as many lives as it would take to achieve the moral and mental purification that one needs to reach nirvana's spiritual plane, and end the continuous cycle of birth, misery and death. And he was dismayed by the decision to bury her in the ground. Far better, he believed, to follow Thai Buddhist custom and reduce her body to ashes by fire so her remains might be kept in a ceramic or metal urn as a family memorial. He looked across the casket.

There with the children was Paul, a lanky, craggy, greying man of fifty or so in a light tropical suit in thin blue stripes. The children were in the uniform of Ruam Rudee, the school run by the sisters of the Church of the Holy Redeemer. Meg, thirteen and a slender, flowering image of Madli, wore the blue-grey skirt, short-sleeved white blouse, white ankle socks and low black shoes; Tim, just six and a dark-haired likeness of Paul, wore the boy's version of shorts and short-sleeved shirt, and clung to a little leather school bag. Small as he was, Tim could not see his mother in her casket. Meg's blank gaze never left her.

Somsak's compassion for Madli's family was rudely jarred by renewed energy in the Reverend Ralph's drone. Beatrice had moved behind her husband to block the sun's hot shaft and fan his flushed neck with a church bulletin, and he seemed set on a long service. Sighing inwardly, Somsak scanned the others.

Ward, in a black-stripe model of Paul's suit, looked pensively on Madli; Freddy, a grey linen suit hanging limp on his thin frame, gazed longingly on her; and Jim, hands pressed to his seersucker jacket, seemed to stare at her breasts while Maria, her complexion pale against her black-silk suit, clutched his arm and stared at his profile. His bulk in a flowered Hawaiian shirt, Carl eyed the pair with amusement.

Somsak felt Wilma glance at him, then quickly look away; brushing a fleck of dust from her white-silk suit, she frowned at Betty, who studied a blue sapphire pin on the breast of her very mini frock in yellow Chiang Mai cotton. He saw that Frank, in short-sleeve khaki drills like his own, looked straight ahead and absently chewed gum; and that Jill, spectacular in an orange pant suit and jewelled leather sandals, kept her insolent black eyes on the sagging beams overhead. Only Susan, a pale-blue chiffon dress falling past her knees, appeared to listen to the Reverend Ralph.

And suddenly he stopped, closed the book, and settled his rheumy eyes on Madli's cleavage. Her dress sweat-stained at the armpits and below her heavy breasts, Beatrice dodged the sun's persistent ray and nudged him. He started, cleared his throat, and twirled a forefinger over the casket to indicate that everyone should say farewell to Madli.

Paul lifted Tim into his arms for a last look at his mother, but with a little cry he buried his face in his father's jacket. Throwing Madli a hurried, imploring glance, Paul carried his son out of the church. Meg slowly passed a hand over her mother's face and yellow locks, softly kissed her cold lips, and followed her father outside.

Ward sent Madli a long, regretful smile. Betty bent an elbow and wiggled her fingers. Susan crossed herself. Wilma unconsciously tried to pull the cocktail dress higher on Madli's breasts. Frank squeezed a slender hand that rested below the breasts, allowing it to slip to her side when he let go. Somsak replaced it, chilled by its clamminess.

Pausing at the doorway as Jim and Maria brushed past to join the others in the shade of the church, he watched Carl give the casket a casual pat, and Freddy clasp one of Madli's hands, press it to his lips, and set it on the casket rim.

Now Jill, her rich perfume defeating the tired smell of decaying wood and mortar, her gaze intense and her lips moving in silent expression, enclosed Madli in her aura once more; and from memory Somsak pictured them bathing nude off a moonlit beach at Hua Hin, dancing barefoot by the pool at the staid Erawan Hotel, absorbing Prince Prem's lush gardens at Samsaen, and hand in hand in dense crowds at the Sunday market by the Temple of the Emerald Buddha in old Bangkok. Splendid foreign women in colourful dress, casting spells wherever they went. Lawless creatures, in his mind.

Once Jill had left, Beatrice signalled and the Chinese undertaker, in yellow shirt, blue shorts and rubber thongs, trotted from the shadows, his gold teeth shining in the light. Behind came his helper, a scrawny, aged Chinese in baggy shorts, tattered brown singlet and bare feet, the casket lid balanced upside down on his bald dome. Taking the ends, Beatrice and the Reverend Ralph flipped it over and held it steady while the undertaker guided its lugs into the casket hinges. She kept the lid ajar as the Reverend, crouching, peering, moved Madli's hand from the rim to her breast, his fingers narrowly escaping when the lid suddenly slammed shut. While she sealed the casket, he rounded up Carl, Ward, Freddy and Jim to carry it outside.

By time they got it there, Paul had led the women and children to the street, and Frank had backed in a pick-up truck, its doors bearing the hands-across-the-sea emblem of AID, the American International Development agency. Sliding the casket into the rear box, they fastened the tailgate, and Frank drove the truck out of the compound, parking ahead of Madli's white Citroen.

Paul was at the Citroen's wheel, the children beside him and Freddy and Wilma in the back. Next were Ward and Betty in his green MG, her mini riding high on wonderful bare legs; Jim in his big red Mercedes with Maria pressed close and Carl and Susan well apart in the rear; then Jill, alone and queenly in her silver Porsche.

Shouting in Thai for their servants to close the compound gates, Beatrice and the Reverend Ralph joined Frank in the truck cab; as the convoy moved off, Somsak started his Lambretta scooter and brought up the rear.

At the corner, a red light stalled them under the grins and stares of loungers outside a bar. On the green they turned left into heavy traffic on Silom, a six-lane road with a concrete centre strip. A few blocks and they were at the Chinese cemetery's high stone wall. As the curb lane was torn up for repairs, they parked in the centre lane and crossed the diggings on planks put down by the cheerful labourers, barefoot women in black shirts and sarongs, and straw coolie hats perched on top of the red kerchiefs tied under their chins. Grinning broadly and chattering noisily, they jostled one another to touch the foreign women and children who followed the men and Madli's casket into the cemetery. Its heavy wooden gates closed on a bedlam of horns and police whistles as swarms of cars, cabs, trucks and buses competed for the remaining traffic lane.

Haste drove the Reverend Ralph's final word when they lowered Madli into her grave in the section reserved for *farangs*, the white foreigners; perspiring freely, his feelings hurt, he stood at the mercy of the cruel sun, for no help came from Beatrice this time. She sheltered with the others under large temple umbrellas held by grimy diggers in black Chinese pyjama pants, her eyes closed to his look of reproach since she was lost in prayer. Quickly committing Madli to heaven, he led the party out of the cluttered grounds before the first earth thudded onto her coffin.

Again Somsak was last. He walked slowly, thinking of all that Madli's servant, Alun, had told him of the happenings on the night and morning of her death.

Madli had spent the evening at home; two hours after Meg and Tim went upstairs to bed around ten, she retired to her room across the hall from theirs; Alun then closed and locked all window shutters and outside doors and withdrew to her room off the adjoining courtyard. Madli liked to spend time with the children before school, so at six-thirty in the morning, after opening the ground-floor doors and window shutters, Alun took Madli her usual wake-up coffee on a tray.

Slivers of light, sifted through cracks in the window shutters, showed dimly that Madli was naked, the way she always slept, that a sheet covered her lower legs and her long hair covered the pillow. Laying the tray on a table, she opened the shutters, and turned to waken Madli as daylight streamed in. Now the terrifying sight of her twisted features, the wound in her left breast, the blood on her silk sheets.

Alun screamed, then sobbed and shook so with fear that all became a blur. She sensed that Meg was suddenly there, kneeling by the bed, kissing her mother's lips, touching her hair, whispering something; and that Meg quickly rose, pulled her into the hall, closed the door, held her till she quietened, then told her to phone Captain Somsak at his home while she comforted little Tim, who cowered in his bedroom doorway and whimpered from fright.

Somsak was at the house soon after seven. To shield his investigation, he threatened to banish Alun to her village in the impoverished North-East if she repeated what she knew to anyone else. When Paul flew in from Saigon, summoned by a tearful phone call from Wilma, and burdened by grief and the arrangements for his wife's funeral, he seemed satisfied with the bare details of her death.

Somsak told the newspapers no more than he had to: Madli had been shot to death some time after midnight and the weapon had not been found. Right away the papers concluded that a *kamoy*, the ubiquitous and ruthless Thai burglar, had broken into the house, entered Madli's bedroom, and killed her when she awoke and confronted him.

And after many hours over many drinks, and much unrestrained conjecture that Madli had been murdered by a jealous and vengeful wife, mistress, or former lover, most of those at her farewell had seemed content to dismiss their suspicions and accept the newspapers' swift judgement.

To Somsak, mulling over the circumstances he had kept to himself, her death remained wrapped in mystery. And prompted by what he knew of her conduct, her companions, and the dangerously loose lives in *farang* circles, he left the cemetery with an uneasy feeling that the most likely suspects in her murder could very well turn out to be the friends and lovers who escorted Madli to her grave.

Chapter Two

"Really, Madli looked simply gorgeous. And so tastefully prepared. A touch of make-up, one bit of jewellery, her lovely hair brushed and glowing on a velvet pillow. A picture of perfection, thanks loads to Meg's supervision. Oh, and that darling frock. One of your creations, Jill?...JILL?!"

"Hang on, Betty! Every glass empty at once. Dammit! Where's that bloody Alun? Wilma takes her in after Madli dies and she's off on her new gossip rounds when she's needed here. That's gratitude for you. Now look, everyone. I am not Wilma's barmaid. Here's the liquor, ice and mix. The Lord helps those who help themselves. You were saying, Betty?"

"Madli's dress. One of yours?"

"Yes, but weeks old. I whipped it up for the national day reception at the Vietnamese embassy. The only time she wore it. Knowing Madli, I felt it was the sort of thing she'd want to be seen in on this occasion."

"I'd love a dress like that if I had the nerve to wear a mini."

"My dear Susan. Only Madli had the figure for it."

"Indeed she did."

"You should know, Ward."

"A classic figure. Quite rare these days."

"How did you find it?"

"Alive and responsive, Jim."

"He knows."

"Can it, Maria."

"So does Frank, and Carl -"

"Shut up, Maria."

"- and Freddy and Jill and -"

"SHUT UP MARIA!"

"That's enough, you two. No point in going on like that after what's happened. For heaven's sake drink up and make up."

"Where the hell you been, Wilma?"

"Freshening up, Frank. Funerals shatter me. Especially those of dear, dear friends like Madli... This my drink? I can use it. Cheers! everyone."

"Sing somethin', Wilma."

"Carl, really, I've just sat down."

"Song's in order."

"What can we possibly sing about today?"

"Madli."

"Madli...?"

"I wonder who killed her?"

"My dear Frank. We went over that for hours. I'm sure it was one of those dreadful *kamoys*."

"I don't know so much."

"Lay off. Time for music. Come on, Wilma."

"Oh, all right, Carl. Why not? The guitar, Betty. There, by that lamp table... Thank you, dear. Now let's see... How about something like this...? All of our days, we'll miss dear Madli,
> we'll miss her beauty,
> we'll miss her laughter,
> we'll miss her loving..."

Somsak smoked, sipped Scotch, and listened. He felt at ease; he knew these people, and he knew Wilma's large, square living room.

The outer walls had wide screen windows that came below the waist, and the back wall also had a screen door to the garden. The inner wall, which he faced, was all vertical tamarind planks in their natural yellow. To his right was the door to Wilma's plush bedroom and bathroom; to his left, an open doorway into a covered courtyard with the dining room, kitchen and servant quarters off it. Between was a long teak buffet, and on the planks above it, half a dozen rubbings of Thai temple carvings. At the front of the room, an open wooden staircase, with an iron railing and two-step landings at top and bottom, led to bedrooms and bathrooms on the second floor; and under its top landing a panelled door opened onto a brick path to a tall iron gate in the high stone wall around the grounds.

There were coconut mats scattered over the polished wood floor, small tables with lamps by the outer walls, a record player and its speakers under the stairs, and a wobbly electric fan and two lamps in Japanese paper-ball shades hanging from the ceiling. The coffee table in the centre of the room was a long slab of thick teak on a big block of granite; and fanning out around it, from a five-cushion sofa opposite the buffet, were three easy chairs, four chairs of yellow bamboo with wide seats of blue Chiang Mai cotton, and several bulky cushions of the same material in shades of red, green and purple.

Wilma's rented house was in one of the nicer districts favoured by *farangs*. Frank had led the way there from the cemetery, and drinks had been poured before Somsak parked his Lambretta behind Jill's Porsche. He had hung his uniform cap among the jackets on the hooks under the stairs, and left his shoes by the door as everyone but Beatrice, the children and the Reverend Ralph had done. She had steered them down the room and into the garden, the Reverend whisking two bottles of beer from a cooler that Alun set up before anybody arrived.

Paul, his tie loosened, now sat hunched over a bottle of Scotch in an easy chair to the left of the stair landing. On the opposite side of the circle, Freddy slumped in an easy chair with a bottle of gin. Neither seemed aware that others sat around or moved about, and that Wilma plucked her guitar and sang softly of Madli.

"Somsak, grab this drink before I pour it in your pocket."

He started, grinned, and took the glass from Betty; she put his empty on the table and turned to Wilma: "Let's have a verse about the hearse. Can you imagine your ambassador's face if he had seen Madli going to her grave in one of Uncle Sam's gifts to the Thai? We know there's not a proper hearse in Bangkok, Frank, but really!"

"I might've borrowed an army half-track instead."

She hooted. "Now that would have made a marvellous picture. Yet I must say the truck gave her funeral a Chinese flavour, except we didn't ride in back and beat drums and gongs over the corpse as they do."

"You could have covered that silly hands across the sea symbol on the doors," Jill said. "Foreign aid is such a waste, and you Yanks get precious little thanks for it."

"Dear Betty," said Wilma, putting aside the guitar, "I liked your piece about Madli in the World this morning. Such a relief from those shocking Thai papers with their gruesome pictures of the poor soul. Somsak, why do you allow it?"

"We think it's a sobering lesson for people to see the results of brutal crimes that might have been prevented. Our custom, Mrs. Wilma."

"Good Lord. Anyway, Betty, thank you for mentioning her close friends and how dear she was to us."

"Glad you liked it. I felt I hadn't done her justice."

"Don't feel badly," said Ward. "Only poetry could do Madli justice. 'Ode to a goddess of love', we might call it. What say, Jim?"

"He'd help compose it," Maria snapped.

"Forget it," Jim murmured.

"When you refused to forget her?"

"We were friends. Everything else was dead."

"Liar! But she is, thanks to someone or other."

"Why, you little - !"

"Please!" Susan begged. "Madli is gone. You have each other. Don't hurt yourselves over the past."

"Take this down, somebody," Jill drawled. "A great idea for soap opera."

"Stickin' Madli in the ground was no great idea," said Carl. "Should've been cremated. That place is a swamp in the rainy season. Her coffin could come apart, for fuck's sake."

"It's teak and pretty tough," said Frank. "The best you can get here. You should see what they're makin' Stateside, though. Friend of mine saw a steel coffin in Miami. It had a thick layer of asphalt between the metal and a lining of pure mink. Cost thirty grand."

"Wow!" said Betty. "But why would anyone want to bury somebody in a thoroughly fortified coffin?"

Ward grinned. "So when they drive past the cemetery on a cold, wet day, they can feel assured that their loved one is snug in a nice strong box under the turf."

"Should've been cremated," Carl growled.

"Cremation here takes time," said Wilma. "It must be done the Thai Buddhist way. I have heard that bodies lie for days in a big pile of firewood in a temple compound while friends and relatives, and even complete strangers, traipse around it or sit looking at it. When a priest decides the moment is right, everybody pokes a flaming stick into the pile to get it burning. Paul had Madli buried to get it over with quickly. But we can still cremate her, if you like. Some

Chinese in Thailand bury their dead by Chinese custom, then dig them up after a while and cremate them by Thai custom. Isn't that right, Somsak?"

"Quite right, Mrs. Wilma," he agreed, feeling amused by her loose description of a Thai cremation, but relieved by her suggestion that Madli might still be cremated.

"Sounds like some sort of weird ritual," said Ward. "But perhaps it's best if we're going to worry about Madli being where she is. We can have her spend eternity in a handsome urn instead." He twinkled. "Do you know, a family friend in England kept his wife's urn on the mantelpiece. A rather touching gesture, but it had a drawback. His pals persisted in using the urn as an ashtray, and now and then one would casually remark that his dearly departed seemed to be putting on a bit of weight... God's truth, I swear."

Betty giggled. "I'll believe you where thousands wouldn't."

"Another thing," said Frank. "Madli was buried by a Protestant minister. I thought she was Roman Catholic."

"Paul's Catholic," said Wilma; she looked to him for confirmation but he kept his eyes on his glass. "Well, he was when we were all together in Saigon. And the children go to a Catholic school. I'm not sure about Madli..."

"Madli worshipped her own god," Jill murmured. "The god of sensual pleasure."

The garden screen door swung open and in came the children, Beatrice and the Reverend Ralph; he held two empty beer bottles above their heads and looked inquiringly towards the open cooler which now contained only water from the melted ice.

"More in the fridge out in the kitchen, your holiness," Betty said sweetly.

"Well..." He glanced at Beatrice; she fussed with the children, helping Tim take off his shoes and arranging cushions for them by their father's chair. "It is terribly hot and thirsty, isn't it?" he said gravely, quickly disappearing into the courtyard.

"Meg," said Jill sharply. "Your brother has carried that God damn school bag around for hours. Tell him to put it away."

Tim clutched the bag and stared solemnly at Jill.

"It's all right, Tim," said Meg softly; and to Jill: "Aunt Wilma told us to bring our books and things so we can go to school from here on Monday."

Wilma nodded. "I think the school routine will help them through their grief over their mother's death."

"It's only Saturday," Jill persisted. "Will he be taking the bloody thing to bed with him?!"

"Who cares if it goes to the fuckin' can with him too?" Carl muttered.

She tossed back her drink. "It irritates. Every damn kid irritates."

"If they turn queer like you they do."

"Swine! Do you think women are put on earth just for your filthy bloody pleasure?!"

"You God damn right!"

"Jesus! It makes me ill to think of Madli with the likes of you!"

"She loved it, spook. She really loved -"

"Ralph!" Wilma broke in as he appeared in the courtyard doorway with a tall glass of beer and a blob of foam on his ruddy nose. "Frank thinks Madli was Roman Catholic, and wonders why she wasn't buried as one."

"Really?" His eyebrows arched and he glanced at Paul, who was still absorbed in his drink. "Did anybody know if Madli had a particular faith? I gather she went along with Paul's beliefs for the children's sake. However, she displayed a great interest in our church. I thought it was only right that I should commit her to heaven."

"And have a good feel of that luscious corpse," Betty murmured.

Susan gasped. "What did you say, Betty?"

"I said Ralph has good Christian feelings," she replied earnestly.

He smiled warmly. "Thank you, Betty. I have always fulfilled my duties to my faith and my church. And I know in my heart that our dear Madli is with her Maker." He drained his glass and headed for the kitchen without a glance at Beatrice.

"With her maker," Carl slowly repeated. "A good pun, if you don't mind."

"Your mind is the least complicated in this room," Wilma said. "It's always on the same track."

He grinned. "I have a joke -"

"I HAVE A QUESTION!" Paul was on his feet, holding on to an arm of his chair and trying to focus on the group.

"Well," said Jill scornfully. "The poor injured husband is heard from at last."

Betty giggled, Frank chuckled, laughter spread among Madli's friends.

"LET HIM SPEAK!"

The laughter swiftly died and looks of surprise were drawn to Freddy; he too was on his feet, dangling a glass of gin and an empty bottle.

"You make me retch!" he said disdainfully. "You have no respect for the dead. No respect for little children or a man of God. For Christ's sake try to show compassion for this grieving husband and father!"

He teetered. "What is it, Paul, old man?" he wheedled. "What is your question?"

Meg touched her father's arm. "Daddy..."

Taking her hand, he pulled himself erect, blinking, his lips quivering:

"WHICH ONE OF YOU ROTTEN BASTARDS MURDERED MY WIFE?!"

Chapter Three

Somsak strolled in Wilma's garden to the sounds of faint, plaintive chords from her guitar and the fainter cries of children at play down her *soi*, the street in front of the high stone wall. Her two-storey house of unpainted teak was off to one side of the compound. Along the wall on the other side were thick banana trees with fronds of brilliant green and clusters of fat dwarf bananas; and tall coconut palms, their trunks encircled by wide strips of greased tin to prevent rats from climbing to the fruit. The bottom of the garden was taken up by a large *klong*, or pond, dotted with slender white water lilies and the broad green leaves of night-blooming lotus. From there to the front wall lay a manicured lawn, its monotony broken here and there by leafy shrubs and beds of tropical flowers in a riot of colours.

By the side of the house, an arbour of white lattice enclosed a red-brick terrace, and from the overhead lattice hung small clay pots of orchids, their luxurious flower in subtle shades of purple. Somsak lingered here. Orchids were his passion. His own pots hung in a low open living space between the concrete stilts of his small wooden house in Lumpini police compound, and they annoyed his wife when she absentmindedly bumped her head on one. He teased her over her poor luck with bougainvillaea, which cascaded across Wilma's arbour and climbed the house to its green-tile roof, their white, red and coffee-coloured petals bright against the dry wood.

He looked to the pale sky. The sun was retreating in a thin veil of misty orange. Soon the nightly armies of ravenous mosquitoes would invade, the lotus in the *klong* would flower at their usual hour, and the nocturnal jasmine's heady scent would blend with the soft, languorous air.

He sniffed. A mouth-watering aroma of simmering, garlicky curry and frying shrimp and fish wafted from Alun's kitchen. His stomach rolled; he hadn't eaten since breakfast and here it was almost seven. By now his wife and children would have had dinner, and he might have been with them but for Paul's outburst.

The effort sent him reeling back into his chair, eyes closed, chin lolling on his chest, hands hanging limp between his splayed thighs.

Then Freddy, arms flailing and gin splashing from his glass, collapsed into his chair. "Poor devil," he whimpered, squinting in Paul's direction. "Is he dead?"

"Bombed is all," said Frank, peeling Paul's eyelids back.

"Party pooper," Jill drawled.

"Bloody cheek!" Betty huffed. "Suggesting that one of us murdered his wife!"

"It was an accusation," said Ward, drawing slowly on his cigar.

"I'm sure Paul didn't mean it," said Susan. "He's under a terrible strain. The shock of Madli's death, dealing with the police and her funeral, and trying to comfort his children." She gazed compassionately on Meg and Tim; they pressed close to their father's chair as he settled into a soft snore.

"I think he meant it," said Ward thoughtfully. "He believes one of us killed his wife."

"Then cut him off," Jill said. "I can't stand morbid drunks."

"Why should Paul care?" Maria humphed. "He was out of the picture. She was falling into bed with every other Tom, Dick, Harry and Jim."

"Leave her be," Jim said quietly.

"Paul did care," said Beatrice timidly. "Madli was his wife and the mother of his children. He loved her..."

"Violins, please," Jill mocked.

"...and he must have prayed that she would come back to him one day."

Jill laughed. "In that case he's insane."

"He must be," said Betty, "or he wouldn't think that one of us killed Madli. He knows us, for heaven's sake."

"Precisely," said Ward; he looked quizzically around the room. "Did one of us kill Madli?"

"It's unthinkable, Ward," said Wilma uneasily.

"Perhaps, but an interesting question all the same. Did one of us kill Madli?"

"That's what I would like to know," Freddy slurred, struggling back to his feet.

"So would I," said Somsak mildly.

"Stay out of this, Somsak," Jill snapped. "It's none of your business."

"I'm afraid it is. I must bring Mrs. Madli's killer to justice."

"And spoil your record?" Carl scoffed.

"My record...?"

"The Brennam murder for starters," Carl said. "You know fuckin' well Prince Srithai shot him because he stole his favourite bum boy. But Srithai gets away with it by bribin' your cops to plant the murder pistol on a *kamoy* they kill in a gun fight. Everybody in Bangkok must know that."

"And the French teacher at International School," Jim put in. "You say he shot himself when his Thai chick ran off. Nobody believes that. He was killed in a fight over the girl and you covered because the killer's the son of a Thai general."

"Yeah," said Frank. "And nobody believes a Chinese sailor robbed and killed that Polish trade attaché and just vanished. The Pole was stealin' his country blind, and he was killed for cheatin' the crooked customs officers he worked with. They paid the police to blame some phoney sailor."

Somsak shrugged. "We solved those cases to our satisfaction. Now we must solve this one."

"Hang on," said Betty. "I thought we agreed that Madli was murdered by a *kamoy*."

"The police haven't mentioned *kamoys*, Miss Betty."

"Sounds like we're all suspects," Carl muttered.

Somsak glanced around apologetically.

"Really, Somsak," Wilma said reproachfully. "We're your friends."

"Routine, Mrs. Wilma. That's all. I'll want to know where you were when Mrs. Madli died. And about your relations with her. Motive, you understand."

"Then let's get it over with," said Ward cheerfully, plopping himself down on the sofa. "Fire away, Captain!"

"Here and now?!" Jill questioned.

"Why not? It's convenient. Accounting for ourselves at one go could make it easier for Somsak to get at the truth."

"And our skeletons in the closet," she added tartly.

"We'll see."

"I can't believe this," said Susan. "Are we actually thinking of looking for Madli's killer among ourselves? It's absurd. We loved her."

"Did we...?"

"I most definitely did!" Freddy insisted.

"And I," said Ward soberly. "I loved her quite deeply. But love has no remedy against dangerous doubts or jealousy. Sometimes they trigger violence."

"And sometimes," Betty said quietly, "those hours of Madli's death, the witching time of night, as Shakespeare called it, are difficult to account for."

"It might be difficult to account for our relations with her as well. But we're friends, Betty. We should try to clear the air, and ourselves of suspicion."

"Might be fun," she said faintly.

He grinned. "Better than dirty word scrabble."

"Really," said Maria warily, moving to Jim's side. "What could we tell about ourselves and Madli that would be of any interest or help?"

"A hell of a lot," said Freddy.

"I'll be surprised if it's news to me," Wilma said. "But even so I wonder if it's wise to air everything?" She sighed. "Oh well. I suppose it's all right if we think it would dispel this awful cloud we seem to be under." She glanced around. "Are we all game...?"

Carl shrugged indifferently. Maria looked closely at Jim and he turned away. Frank grimaced and stared at his glass. Susan and Beatrice exchanged an unsettled glance, Freddy grinned inanely, and Meg touched her father's arm as though to draw his attention. Somsak lit another cigarette.

"This is stupid!" said Jill, shaking her head impatiently. "It plays right into the hands of this cop. We could regret it." She glared at Ward. "You and your bright ideas. But go ahead. What the hell, there's not a damn thing about Madli and me that I would want to hide."

"Let's get on with it then," he said easily.

"Hold it!" she said quickly. "I refuse to confess to murder on an empty stomach. We eat first." She turned towards the courtyard doorway. "Alun! Get in here!" There was no response. "Where's that bloody girl...? ALUN!"

Suddenly a short, slight and darkly pretty woman appeared in the doorway, frantically straightening her white blouse and black sarong. "Madam call?" she asked nervously, looking uncertainly from Wilma to Jill.

"Of course 'madam call', you little idiot," Jill scolded. "Now hustle back to that kitchen and rustle up dinner. Make lots of dinner, you hear? *Reho-reho*! - quickly!"

Nodding vigorously, Alun pulled up her sarong and scurried away, her bare feet padding on the courtyard tiles.

Jill chuckled. "Like I put a firecracker up her ass..." She surveyed the room. "Christ. What a mess. Girls, get the empties and ashtrays. Boys, get lost."

"Frank," said Wilma. "While we're waiting for dinner you could round up more PX booze. Seems everything's gone but the beer."

"Thanks to the Bobbsey twins," Jill said, jerking her head towards Paul, dead to the world in his chair, and Freddy, who looked as if he was rooted in front of his. "They were half sloshed before we buried Madli."

"What should we do with them?" Betty asked, a full ashtray in each hand.

"Dump them in the garbage," said Wilma.

"I mean Paul and Freddy."

"You heard what the lady said," Jill cracked.

"A cold shower'll do the trick," said Carl. "Grab his other arm, Jim."

The children stepped back and watched silently as they pulled their father to his feet, draped his arms over their shoulders and carried him, toes dragging, down the room and through the door to Wilma's bedroom and bathroom.

"You forgot something!" Jill called.

Freddy drew himself up. "I can take care of myself, thank you," he said haughtily. Striking out towards the bedroom, he stumbled, lurched forward, and scraped through the open doorway. Susan closed the door after him.

"Good riddance, for a while anyway," Jill said. "They give drinking a bad name." Then briskly: "Now then, what say we eat buffet style? Maria, when you take those empties to the kitchen, bring back a bunch of plates, paper napkins, forks, spoons -"

"Can I be of some help?" the Reverend Ralph enquired cheerfully, entering the room with a bottle of beer and a benign smile, his old school tie askew and his shirt buttons strained over his paunch.

"You can help decorum," said Betty, "by zipping up your fly."

Beatrice winced and looked away as he followed Betty's gaze to the shirt tail peeping from his trousers; mumbling confusedly, he quickly about turned and retreated to Alun's kitchen.

"Susan!" Jill ordered. "Get the hell out there and see what's cooking."

"What...?"

"Park yourself in the kitchen and keep that little nympho's mind on dinner or we'll never eat tonight."

Smiling to herself, Susan picked up a couple of empty bottles and trailed Maria into the courtyard as Jill levelled a finger at Frank:

"The booze, soldier. Get the lead out, dammit!"

He grinned and knocked back his drink. "Coming, Ward? We can pick up some records at my place as well."

"Righto!" said Ward exuberantly, emptying his glass and jumping up from the sofa. "I can do with an outing, by golly."

Putting on the shoes they had left under the stairs, they stepped out the front door and shut it behind them; immediately it opened a little and Ward poked his head in:

"Don't go away, Somsak. Save us some rice, Wilma. Wait for me, Betty." He returned her grin and closed the door.

"Sweet boys," Wilma murmured; and to Beatrice: "There are bathrooms off the bedrooms upstairs, my dear. Perhaps you and the children would like to freshen up before dinner. Little Tim is falling asleep on his feet."

"Thank you, Wilma," she said. "We are tired and hungry. It's been a long day. Come along, children."

Pulling the strap of his school bag over his shoulder, Tim took Meg's hand and they started up the stairs behind Beatrice.

"Meg, dear..."

She paused, a hand on the iron railing and her blue eyes on Wilma.

"Are you all right? You look rather drawn."

"I'm okay, Aunt Wilma."

"Remember, child, your mother would want you and Tim safe among friends. You have nothing to fear."

"Yes, Aunt Wilma. I know."

She watched them disappear up the stairs and sighed. "I'm not used to having children around. I do hope I can manage." Squirming into a comfortable position in the easy chair, she placed the guitar in her lap and began to pluck its strings, singing quietly to herself:

> "All of our days
> we'll miss dear Madli ...

"Jill, there's a good heel in that gin bottle by the table. Fix us both a drink, will you, darling? I have such a thirst ...

> "we'll miss her laughter,
> we'll miss her kisses..."

Returning from the kitchen with plates, forks, spoons and paper napkins, Maria arranged them on the buffet, softly humming to the melody; and Betty, stretching out on the sofa, closed her eyes and smiled at the muffled sounds of running water and bits of laughter from Wilma's bathroom.

Now Jill, after balancing a glass of gin and tonic on an arm of Wilma's chair, curled up with her own drink on a big puffy cushion at her feet, and listened dreamily to her lament:

> "We'll miss her loving
> now she's far away..."

It was at that moment when Somsak picked up his shoes at the front door, carried them down the room to the screen door, put them on, and quietly slipped into the garden.

CHAPTER FOUR

"Captain Somsak."

He whirled instinctively.

"Sorry," said Susan. "I didn't mean to startle you."

He smiled. "It's all right. I was daydreaming."

"Dinner is almost ready. Hungry?"

"Famished. And you?"

"Yes. I'm sure everybody is. And there's lots to eat. Alun made shrimp curry, pilaff, *plakaplong* fish with sweet and sour sauce, and mountains of steamed rice. Smells yummy."

He inhaled deeply. "At this moment I prefer it to the perfume of the jasmine."

She gazed around her. "Wilma has such a lovely garden. And so private and peaceful."

"I especially like her orchids. One is quite rare. I must ask her for a shoot."

"Have you a large garden?"

"By no means. It's very small. Our house is in the Lumpini police compound. My few orchids hang in pots in the open space below it, and my wife tries to persuade bougainvillaea to climb the concrete stilts, though she has little success."

"She must be wondering where you are."

"Perhaps. But she is used to my strange hours."

"Why have we not met her? Why don't you bring her to our parties?"

"It's not proper for Thai men to take their wives to *farang* parties."

She looked at him closely. "You don't want her to meet us, do you?"

"But why...?"

"I'm not sure," she said, her eyes clouding. "Is it because you don't like us?"

"Miss Susan! really –"

"Let me explain, Somsak. It's nearly five years since I began teaching English in Thailand. I know many Thai, some quite well. But I don't have an intimate Thai friend. Oh, yes, your young men would be only too happy to be my 'friend', as they keep telling me. You know what they mean. It's quite a feather in their cap if they can boast of the conquest of a blonde *farang* in the shameful way they discuss their Thai girl friends. No thanks. I'd just like to have a Thai as a close friend, the sort I grew up with. I try, but I can get only so far, then I'm up against a subtle barrier that keeps us out of your homes and your lives, and seems to tell me what you really think of us."

He shook his head. "We don't dislike you," he said candidly. "We don't understand you. Even I find it difficult in spite of the years I spent studying English and police methods in the West. Getting to know your customs and lifestyles was no problem. Yet I could never penetrate your characters. They're entirely foreign to us, so we keep a certain...distance. Still, many Thai get along famously with *farangs*. Myself for one."

"You must. Dealing with *farangs* is your job. Other police leave us to stew in our own juice."

"Wisely, I think."

"Perhaps... We do intrude, many of us. Sometimes I think the Thai wish that everybody would go home." She gazed pensively at the house. "Strangers, even after years among you. So we gather like this."

"What keeps you here?" he asked softly.

She shrugged. "Many of the things that keep others here. The living's easy. Gardens like this year round. The warm sun. The sea close by. Your wonderful fruits, flowers, festivals. Your peaceful temples and sleepy monks. Your graceful manners and dancers. And yes, your eternal smiles too, darn it, and your careless, carefree approach to all things, exasperating as it is." She paused, then earnestly: "And something very personal, Somsak. When I was alone and adrift and did not know where to turn, your country gave me sanctuary and purpose. I'm grateful, and content. I owe you that." And smiling faintly: "An odd lot, aren't we? Many *farangs* I know spend half their time griping and wishing they were somewhere else, yet they find all sorts of excuses for staying on."

There was a burst of laughter from the house; he smiled. "You seem to enjoy yourselves."

"Do we?"

"Well, you like to get together for a drink and a bit of fun."

"I suppose..."

"And you like to complain about my country. It's too hot, too dry, too humid. It's perilous with poisonous snakes, mosquitoes, venereal disease and murderous *kamoys*. My people are lazy, corrupt, larcenous, inefficient -"

"And the police take bribes to look the other way," she teased.

"Exactly. We have just heard some typical *farang* contempt for Thai police and Thai justice."

"Were they quite wrong?"

"Miss Susan, it's up to the courts to decide guilt and punishment. The police are not supposed to meddle with that, yet they do. Everywhere. For example, police connive with prosecutors in offering an accused person a lighter sentence in exchange for a confession, or help in catching an accomplice. We meddle in other ways as well..."

He looked at her quizzically. "I trust you'll keep this to yourself...?" She nodded, and he went on: "The French teacher's wife was driven out of her mind by his brazen affair with the Thai girl. She lost control. We could have charged her with murder, but at what price? She was a broken woman. We called it suicide and she went home to her mother in France. And Mr. Brennam..." His eyes hardened. "We are tolerant of sexual leanings, but he flaunted his homosexuality. He corrupted many young Thai and procured for homosexual friends from abroad. He was shot by the grieving father of a boy he seduced and passed around. We felt he had it coming. But our friends had one thing right. We did plant the murder weapon on a *kamoy* who was killed in a gunfight with police. Miss Susan, I think we took the right step in both cases."

She nodded sympathetically. "I think many would agree. The versions in there were from the *farang* rumour and gossip mill. I've heard them before. They also brought up the murder of the Polish trade attaché, if you remember."

"Yes, but I had nothing to do with that case, oddly enough. It was a higher authority that said he was robbed and killed at Klong Toey port by a Chinese seaman who quickly disappeared, and is believed to have fled the country."

"A higher authority...?"

"I can say no more. I told you how we handled those other cases so you might see us in a different light."

"I understand," she said. "Many expatriates tend to distrust the police in some countries. We forget that those at home are not all upstanding. Back in Regina, we had a terrifying case of police persecution against a young man who charged an officer with assault."

"Regina, Saskatchewan. I have been there."

"I can't believe it!"

He laughed. "Ten years ago. For two weeks. I was in Washington studying FBI methods, and they sent me to a special course at the Royal Canadian Mounted Police crime laboratory in Regina. It's quite famous. But I saw very little of your city. It was winter, all snow and freezing cold. I preferred the warmth of the Mounties' barracks."

"You didn't miss much. I was born and raised in Regina. In early autumn, on the plains round about, ripe wheat stretches from one flat horizon to another. It's a lovely gold, the only beauty I can remember. Yet all too soon the harvest reduces the fields to ugly stubble. Then it's winter again, that awful winter. Regina is one reason I live a world away from Canada."

"One reason, yes."

She looked at him uncertainly. "You know...?"

He nodded. "It will never go further."

She drew a tremulous breath. "I regret what I did, Somsak. I felt justified at the time. The boy I had loved since high school turned his back on me when I got pregnant, so I couldn't bear the thought of having his child. But it was my child too, and I should have considered that. I had the abortion in Japan, then came to Bangkok because I was told you needed English teachers, and it was far away from the shame I would have faced at home."

"I'm sorry."

"You know a lot about us, don't you?"

"We can't know everything."

"But you keep dossiers on us obviously."

"Police everywhere keep records on people. Even in Regina."

"Good old Regina."

"It was your home, Miss Susan. Some day you will return, if just for a visit."

"Home," she repeated wistfully. "Many of us don't know its meaning anymore."

"At any rate," he said lightly, "I was in your city when you were a schoolgirl. If I hadn't been afraid of the cold, we might have passed one another in the street. Now here you are, a young woman, living in my country. Surely a basis for understanding...?"

He smiled encouragingly and she nodded, smiling a little in spite of herself. He clicked his heels and offered his arm.

"Shall we join our friends at dinner?"

She hesitated, then slipped an arm in his; halfway to the house, she stopped and faced him: "Why only these people at Madli's funeral and not her many other friends? Why did we not leave Paul and the children in peace afterwards? What are we doing here?"

He put a finger to his lips. "Paul's idea, only these people, and this gathering. He said I might hear something that will help my investigation."

"Have you...?"

"Not yet. It's becoming interesting, though."

"You must know much more about Madli's murder than you let on."

"You will know eventually. Bear with me."

"Paul seems to think that one of us killed her. Is that possible...?"

"We shall see."

She sighed. "I can't imagine any of us being capable of killing her."

"Miss Susan. The veneer between primitive and civilised people is as thin as a razor blade. Unbearable pressure can break it and free our worst instincts. Then we are capable of the foulest crimes. I know, from my years as a policeman."

"So you would not be surprised if you found that it was me who killed Madli. Is that what you're saying?"

He chuckled. "Come. Let's go in before the mosquitoes devour us and our friends devour all the food. That would be a crime."

"Aha!" Jill hooted as the screen door closed behind them. "Old Charley Chan has been grilling a prime murder suspect. Hope you didn't take it lying down, Susan."

"That's the best way," said Carl, leering through a mouthful of rice.

"We were admiring Wilma's garden," Susan said lamely.

"Getting the lay of the land is more like it," said Jill. "How is it when the twain meet?"

"Much like it is with anyone else, I imagine," said Wilma absently.

Betty giggled. "Really, you are a beastly lot. Somsak, Susan, get a plate and help yourselves. The fish is marvellous, but mind the curry. It's blazing hot!"

Chapter Five

The long teak buffet against the wall of tamarind planks was crowded with steaming tureens of pilaff, curry and white rice, platters of fried fish, aromatic dishes of fish sauce, spicy curry condiments and hot peppers in sesame oil, large bowls of fruit, and clusters of PX beer, their cold bottles beaded with sweat in the warm room.

Alun hovered, proud of her dishes and keen to see everyone eat as much as possible.

Paul and Freddy, their hair damp from the shower, had reclaimed their easy chairs at opposite sides of the circle. Paul's was to the left of the lower staircase landing; Meg and Tim were on cushions beside him and Beatrice on a bamboo chair just across the landing. Freddy's was down the room; he had the Reverend Ralph on a bamboo chair on his left and Wilma in her easy chair on his right. Betty and Jill were on cushions at her feet and Carl sat on a bamboo chair between Jill and the buffet.

Taking a seat on either side of Jim and Maria on the wide sofa opposite the buffet, Susan and Somsak stood their beer on the long coffee table in the centre and, like the others, balanced their plate of food on their knees and ate with relish.

Alun, her dark eyes now darting around the circle, beamed at the generous compliments.

"Don't be shy about going for seconds," Wilma said, sucking sweet and sour sauce from a finger. "Alun has made enough to feed a small army."

"She is a marvellous cook," said Susan approvingly.

"Almost worth killing for," said Betty.

"Really, Betty!" Wilma protested.

"Just a funny, old dear."

"Well, it's not very funny under the circumstances. I was looking for a new servant because dear Pook had been wanting to leave so she could keep house, and do other things, I suppose, for one of our young GIs who seem to be stationed in Bangkok by the thousands. And I knew Alun, of course. She had been with Madli ever since we all moved here from Saigon. She's devoted to Meg and Tim. I'm sure Madli would be pleased that I have given her a good home."

"I sure as hell am," said Jim, digging into a third helping of curry and rice. "Mind if I eat here from now on?"

"Where the Jesus are those commandos on the booze mission?" Carl said. "I can stand so much beer, then I gotta have a drink."

"Beer in this heat makes one perspire so," Freddy said wearily, mopping his face and neck with a napkin.

The Reverend Ralph took a swig from his bottle. "I understand beer is good for the system," he remarked piously. "And in the tropics, one must absorb large quantities of liquids to keep the body functioning well."

"Have you tried water?" Jim asked straight-faced.

"You must be joking," said Jill, uncoiling gracefully from her cushion and carrying her plate to the buffet. "Even his baptismal bowl is alcoholic."

"I say!" the Reverend gasped.

"Perhaps Ward has gone to pick up his wife," Maria suggested.

Betty choked on a spoon of pilaff. "Good Lord! Surely not. He told me that Paddi is spending the evening rehearsing another silly play in their flat with that fruity lot from the British Council's school of English. It'll go on for hours, and I can't see Ward going near the place till they've cleared out."

"All the same," said Maria, "Paddi is a very eligible player for Ward's crazy game of find the killer. She had every reason to murder Madli, the way those two carried on."

"A motive shared by others," said Jim laconically, ignoring Maria's glare.

Carl chuckled. "They could do it right under Paddi's nose and that little ice box would figure it's just part of the script."

"Maria has a good point," said Jill, sinking onto her cushion with a plate of papaya. "Why encourage this notion that one of us might have killed Madli?"

"It doesn't have to be one of us," said Susan.

"It does," said Paul abruptly, gripping the arms of his chair to pull himself upright.

"Well I declare," Jill sneered. "Dr. Watson, I presume."

"Please..." For a moment he clamped his eyes shut as if collecting his thoughts. "Hear me out..."

"We're all ears, old chap," said Freddy helpfully.

"Not for more drunken rubbish, I'm not," Betty muttered.

"Never fear," Jill mocked as attention drifted to Paul. "Dear Watson's insane enough to think he has sober reasons for suspecting us."

"I do," he said, clearing his throat once or twice. "And I know what I'm about, believe me... Now, as you know, Alun found my wife shot dead early yesterday morning and the weapon has not turned up. That's all the police would say. My case calls for a complete picture. Listen carefully..." Then glancing briefly at Somsak, and sucking in a shaky breath: "Madli spent the last evening of her life at home with her children. They read and played cards until Meg and Tim went upstairs to bed around ten. At midnight, Madli retired to her upstairs room, a signal for Alun to secure the house. She bolted all window shutters, locked every outside door, and left only a dim night light burning by the front entrance. Then she went to her bedroom off the adjoining courtyard, locking the door to the house behind her."

He drew attention to Alun, listening wide-eyed by the buffet. "She's loyal and dependable. She kept that routine because those bloody *kamoys* are at their worst after midnight. Her morning routine allowed Madli an hour or so with the children before they left for school. First she opened the downstairs doors and window shutters. At six-thirty sharp she took Madli a pot of coffee on a tray, opening her window shutters before waking her. That was the moment when Alun saw Madli lying there dead, and blood on the sheets from a wound in her left breast. Her screams awoke the children..." He winced as he met his daughter's eye. "Poor Meg. A terrible blow to see her mother in that state. Imagine how she must have felt. Yet she managed to calm Alun's hysterics and get her to phone Captain Somsak at his home and tell him what had happened, while she..." Sighing deeply, he touched his son, who tried to hide behind his father's leg. "The commotion frightened Tim. He was at his door in tears. Meg held him, saying their mother had gone to a lovely -"

"Can the kiddy crap and get on with it," Jill snapped.

Returning her glare, he concluded sharply: "Somsak was there in minutes. He found the other window shutters upstairs still bolted, and not a sign anywhere that anyone had even tried to break into the house. So stop blaming a *kamoy* for my wife's murder."

As that sank in he began to pour the last of his bottle of beer into a glass, and Somsak casually caught Alun's eye; she cringed and shook her head rapidly.

"And if it wasn't a *kamoy*... ?" Jim queried.

"It was someone she knew quite well," said Paul, sipping the beer.

"Someone -"

"She let in," Betty tossed in quickly. "By all accounts she often had late callers, so she must have opened her front door to a familiar somebody or other who, for some stupid reason, had come with a gun to do her in. It could have been one of dozens of people Madli knew, and not necessarily any of us."

"It's possible," said Susan.

"But not likely," Paul insisted. "If that were the case she'd be answering the door bell or knocker and greeting her caller, noises that Alun would have heard in her room a few feet away. She was awake till nearly three - a personal matter, I gather - and the police doctor puts Madli's death at around two-thirty. Alun didn't hear a sound and for a damn good reason. The killer was able to steal into that house without disturbing a soul."

"With a key...?" Maria mused, staring at the table.

"With a key," he agreed, eyeing her briefly. "For various reasons Madli had given a key to her house to each of her closest friends. Obviously, one of them is her killer, and I'm sure they shot her with a small pistol I left with Madli in Saigon to defend herself and the children if they were in danger while I was away. She kept the pistol in her bedroom, and it's gone."

He paused, looking slowly round the circle. "The close friends who have a key to that house," he said deliberately, "are yourselves and Frank and Ward."

Madli's friends glanced at one another silently and soberly; and this time when Somsak caught Alun's eye she buried her face in her apron, and he wondered if she had told him everything she knew.

"I get your lousy little game," Carl growled, scowling at Paul. "You make sure we're the only friends at Madli's funeral so you can corner us at Wilma's booze-up afterwards and show this cop why the killer has to be one of us."

"And show us as well," Betty murmured.

"Very clever of you, Paul," said Freddy admiringly. "But one thing puzzles me. Why did that blighter make off with your dear wife's little pistol, do you think?"

"To get rid of evidence, I would say. Madli's pistol probably vanished in the muddy bottom of a *klong* before the night was out. By the way, Somsak, it was a thirty-two."

"The calibre of the bullet we took from her body," he replied evenly.

Jill turned to him like a shot. "Didn't you know about Madli's pistol, Somsak?"

"Not until now," he admitted, smiling slightly to hide his concern over Paul's failure to tell him all he had learned early on.

"And the keys?"

Reluctantly he shook his head and she pounced on Paul: "Sneaky Dr. Watson's after Charley Chan's job. Big mouth. Let the cops do their own dirty work."

"Come now," said Susan. "I'm sure Somsak was aware of the other circumstances Paul mentioned, and he was bound to find out about the keys and the pistol sooner or later."

"Maybe so," said Jill. "But I bet he's surprised that Paul has been gumshoeing around. Christ! I'm surprised he was sober enough to do anything after he flew in from Saigon."

"What do you want of us, Paul?" Wilma sighed.

"Madli's killer, of course," he said bitterly, accepting another beer from Alun. "I want the cruel bastard nailed before it's too late. We can't expect them to be delivered on a platter, but I gather from something Maria said a while ago that Ward has an idea...?"

"A harebrained idea," Jill said scornfully. "He thinks we should try to clear ourselves of suspicion by telling Somsak, right here in front of everybody, all the ins and outs of our relations with Madli and what we were up to when she was murdered. Well, can you imagine?"

"Not a bad idea," he said, glancing at Meg. "Somsak has to pursue those questions anyway. Let's wait till Frank and Ward get back and see what happens."

"I too am beginning to question the wisdom of going along with Ward," Wilma said unhappily.

"Don't you want Madli's murderer caught?" he asked suspiciously.

"Of course," she stammered. "But surely the police can do it without -"

"Not without our co-operation they can't. We are the foreigners. We know what makes us tick and when we lie. I say let's do all we can to help Somsak find which one of you used their key to get into that house and -"

"I don't have a key!" Maria cried.

"You could get hold of a key."

"But I never..." she began, turning anxiously to Jim.

"Paul merely said you have access to my key," he told her. "It's true. Just as you have access to my mail."

"Disgraceful!" Jill snorted, appearing shocked. "I had no idea a mistress prowled through her man's pockets and letters like an ordinary wife."

"I am not his mistress!" Maria stormed. "I come from a good family, I'll have you know!"

"Don't we all?" Betty murmured. "But what's that got to do with anything?"

"Nothing extraordinary about my key," said Wilma. "We were very close, Madli and I. We shared things. She had a key to my house as well. I often popped into her place for something or other when everyone was out."

"The purpose of my key was far more personal," Jill breathed, smiling secretively.

"Want to tell us about it, spook?" Carl asked, grinning lewdly.

"Drop dead, scum!" she spat. "I suppose Madli gave keys to you guys so she could phone one of you to rush over whenever she lay panting in bed for a stud. Christ! Freddy too?" She shuddered and turned to Susan. "You got a key when she let you take her spare bedroom for a while, right?"

Susan nodded. "And I neglected to leave it there when I moved out, though I had no further use for it really."

"I had to have a key," said Betty. "Madli did that fashion page for our Sunday edition and I came to the house for her copy and sketches. It was often locked because Alun was at the market, the children at school, and Madli God knows where. I asked for a key to save trips."

"And we know why Ralph and Beatrice had a key," Wilma said. "They stayed with Meg and Tim when their mother spent a few days by the sea at Pattaya or Hua Hin."

"And when she went to Vientiane," said Beatrice. "Madli liked Vientiane for the French language and atmosphere that lingers from their long occupation of Laos. For the shopping too. She found the prices on French wines, cigarettes, perfumes and lingerie much cheaper than in Bangkok."

"We moved in with the children for the sake of stability," the Reverend said loftily. "All children should have the warmth and security of a constant home life, don't you know."

"And a normal mother and father," Betty gibed.

"Whatever they are," Jill humphed, her eyes on Meg and Tim now as they left their cushions and went to the buffet with their plates. "Why don't you fill that God damn school bag while you're at it?" she jeered.

Tim gripped the bag and pressed against Meg; she put an arm around him and turned to Wilma. "We're getting fruit for Aunt Beatrice and Daddy," she said calmly. "And may Tim and I have a Coke, Aunt Wilma?"

"Of course, dear. Help yourselves from the fridge." They disappeared into the courtyard and she touched Jill's arm. "Don't be hard on them, Jill. They're only children, you know."

"Exactly," she said peevishly, nervously lighting a cigarette. "And so damn infuriating. The boy gives me the creeps. He just looks. He never says anything. Has anyone ever heard him speak?"

"I have," Paul said with a wan smile. "Quite often, in fact."

"Pity poor bloody you," she sneered, exhaling a stream of smoke. "And Meg's snooty bloody attitude. Watching you like a hawk in that house as if you were trying to steal something, for Christ's sake. Shadowing her mother like a God damn warden."

"She looks so much like her mother," said Susan.

Jill snorted. "Her mother was warm, alive, passionate. Her little Satanic majesty is cold, unfeeling. God knows what's behind those empty eyes."

"It's almost ten," said Maria, checking her watch. "Shouldn't they be in bed?"

"They want to be with their father," Beatrice said, smiling gently as Meg and Tim returned with bottles of Coke and began putting fruit on their plates at the buffet. "It's Paul's first visit in weeks. He has only a few days. And everything has been most distressing."

"It's becoming more so," Susan sighed. "I don't think they should be here."

"Madli didn't mind them hanging around," Jill said, her eyes tracking Meg and Tim to their cushions by Paul. "They saw some pretty hairy goings-on in that house."

"Madam! Madam!" Alun piped merrily on her way out the door with an armful of empties. "Beeah all gone!"

"Impossible," Wilma said. "Paul brought us six dozen with all that Scotch and gin last night."

"Madam! Madam!" Betty chirped. "You fwends soak up dwink like gweat big blottah!"

"Where the hell's Frank and Ward?" Carl bitched. "PX booze ain't that hard to find on a Saturday night, for fuck's sake."

Stubbing out her cigarette, Jill stretched her lithe limbs and grimaced. "Just like Ward to piss off after setting up this stupid witch-hunt. All fun and games, that boy." And peering closely at Somsak: "Hey, copper. You're out of your tree if you think one of us will own up to killing Madli. Pin the murder on Alun so we can all go look for a decent party."

He smiled broadly. "I'm sure I know all there is to know about Alun's movements at the time of the crime."

"Her movements, eh?" she snickered. "That little old hot pants. She's probably got a whole platoon of cabbies to back her alibi." Then as if on a whim she nudged Betty's bottom with her toe. "What say we cut out, doll? Narsing's at The Domino tonight. Great music -"

Suddenly her ears pricked up. A vehicle had braked noisily in the *soi;* they heard its doors squeak open and slam shut and voices draw near. "Our lost patrol is back," she whispered. "Mission accomplished, no doubt."

"Alun!" Wilma called. "Bring lots of glasses, ice, water and mix!" She beamed. "Now we can put some cheer into this sad gathering of Madli's dear family and close friends."

Chapter Six

If there was one regrettable consequence of the *farang* invasion of his country that Somsak could not forgive, it was the degradation of so many of its young women.

It sickened him to think of the thousands of girls, mostly from villages and farms, who had been lured or forced into prostitution in Bangkok to please tourists, resident *farangs*, and the swarms of American soldiers and airmen on leave from their bases in Thailand and the war in Vietnam.

But it pained him as much to see any Thai girl in a *farang's* clutches, for he was sure they would soon discard her once another ripe young creature caught their fancy; then she would likely drift in *farang* circles, her youth and beauty resented by the women and her childlike affections callously exploited by the men.

And over the years he had developed a cynical belief that *farang* men saw all young Thai women as mere playthings, and aimed to seduce as many as they could get their hands on. So it was no more than what he might expect, and no surprise to him at least, when Frank and Ward, in high spirits and bearing cases of liquor, were followed through Wilma's front door by two very young and very pretty Thai girls with a few records cradled in their arms.

They were dressed alike: short, sleeveless and low-cut frilly red blouses that displayed tempting portions of small pointed breasts and slim brown tummies; wide black belts looped around white bell-bottom slacks that clung to firm and shapely buttocks; and thin leather sandals with tiny turquoise stones set in their single thong.

And they were adorned much the same: a slight gold necklace, bracelet and ring, and a light touch of lipstick that matched the crimson polish on the nails of their slender fingers and toes. The only difference was in their lustrous black hair; one girl's flowed freely from her narrow shoulders to her little waist, and the other's fell in a long, thick braid from a big yellow bow at her neck.

As they stepped into the light and took in the room of *farangs*, their dark eyes sparkled merrily and their even white teeth gleamed through wide and inviting smiles.

Dropping his case of liquor by the low centre table, Frank accepted the records they carried, put them by the player under the stairs, and wrapped an arm around each girl. They came no higher than the pocket on his khaki shirt.

"Ain't they somethin'?!" he roared.

Carl whistled softly. "I'll take the one in braids."

"I'll take her friend," Jill purred.

Jim brushed off Maria's restraining hand and leaned forward to ogle, Freddy and Paul grinned unconsciously, the Reverend Ralph gaped, Beatrice studied the ceiling, Susan gazed sympathetically at Somsak, and Betty glared accusingly at Ward.

Humming cheerfully, he was taking bottles from a case and setting them up with a flourish among the glasses, bucket of ice cubes, and cans of soda and tonic water that Alun was busy placing on the table.

Recognising Wilma as the matriarch, the girls greeted her respectfully in the Thai manner with a *wai*, their hands pressed together and head slightly bowed as if they prayed.

"*Sawadee*, my dears," said Wilma, returning their *wai*. "But forgive me, should I know you...?"

Frank laughed and squeezed the pair. "You ain't seen 'em before, Wilma." He nuzzled the hair of the girl in braids. "This little doll is Noi, and this one (nuzzling the other) is Dang."

Braids playfully poked a long crimson fingernail into his ribs. "You keep fohget. Me Dang. She Noi."

"We like falang too much," said Noi, smiling happily on the room. "You have bootiful house. We look, hokay?"

Slipping out of Frank's arms and their sandals, they stepped lightly down the room, tight buttocks swaying and their eyes missing nothing, till they came to the open doorway of Wilma's plush bedroom. Peeking inside, they chattered excitedly, and turned with wide grins.

"Fwank!" Dang exclaimed, slender hands on her slim hips. "This you bedwoom? Wewy nice. Dang be wewy hoppy heah."

Frank chuckled, Maria gasped, Betty snorted, Beatrice frowned at the Reverend's mesmerised interest, Somsak stared stonily at his cigarette, and Jim and Carl exchanged knowing grins.

"They must be bar girls," Wilma said faintly.

Noi and Dang looked crestfallen.

"Hostesses," Ward corrected.

They brightened, and sent another melting smile around the room. Spotting the children on their cushions by Paul, they skipped over and knelt and touched them, laughing gaily at Tim's shyness, and listening in wonder to Meg's quiet response in Thai to their flurry of questions.

"Where'd you find 'em?" Carl asked, leaving his chair to pour himself a Scotch on ice.

"At the Dew Drop," said Frank. "Our first watering hole after we left here. I pulled rank to steal 'em away from a couple of GIs. Then we rounded up the booze."

"From some of Frank's air force chums," said Ward. "It wasn't easy. He had to pry it out of them by pledging his PX liquor rations for months to come. But drink up, and thank the Lord that Uncle Sam provides for his warriors' unquenchable thirsts."

"Did Noi and Dang go with you to Frank's for the music?" Betty asked casually, returning to her cushion with a Scotch and soda.

"Ah. The music. And I've got one just for you, Betty." Sipping a neat Scotch, he went to the records and picked one.

"You were at his place for more than an hour, surely."

"It's Brubeck and a favourite of yours, if I'm not mistaken." He placed the record on the turntable and switched on the player.

"Have you forgotten the amusing little game you talked us into? You know, where we all unburden ourselves in front of everybody here so Somsak can decide which one of us was the most likely to have murdered Madli?"

"Not at all. Patience, dear Betty."

Drinks in hand, he and Frank settled on the lower stair landing, their eyes closed to the expressive strains of strings and brass. She lit a cigarette and gazed at him reproachfully.

"Lovely," Wilma breathed, tasting a tall gin and tonic that Jill had fixed for her. "Thanks for the booze and all that jazz, as they say. And seeing what kept you boys, it's a wonder that you made it back here tonight." She beckoned to Noi and Dang; politely excusing themselves, they left the children and came and squatted in front of her, Noi against Jill's cushion and Dang by Betty's. "And now young ladies, why don't you - ?"

"If you will pardon me, please?" Freddy said, abruptly rising from his chair and brushing past the little group to descend on the liquor.

Tucking a bottle of gin and one of Scotch under an arm, he dropped ice cubes into three glasses, picked them up as a cluster with his fingers, and carefully threaded his way to Paul's side. He gave him the Scotch and a glass, murmured 'not at all' to a muffled 'thanks', and returned to his chair. Now grasping the remaining glasses between his knees, he uncapped the gin, filled the glasses, and placed one in the Reverend's waiting hand. He held his own to the light for a moment, twirling the ice around, then drained it and sighed contentedly.

"You fwend wewy tusty," Noi whispered, watching him wide-eyed.

"You ain't seen nothin' yet," Jill drawled. "Pretty soon he gets his booze intravenously."

"Infla...? Inflewly... ?" She straightened, thrusting out her small breasts. "Me come flom Chiang Mai," she said proudly. "Me Chiang Mai guhl."

"Who cares?" Betty muttered.

"Me too Chiang Mai guhl!" Dang chirped, smiling at Betty. "You like Chiang Mai guhl?"

"Only when they're in Chiang Mai."

Noi touched Betty's arm; she jerked it away and reached for an ashtray near Jill. Noi smiled. "You wewy bootiful. You wewy good. Same same Noi."

"Same same Dang too!" Dang chimed in.

"Cheeky little bitches," Betty huffed.

"Don't take offence, Betty," said Susan. "You can be sure none was meant. It's their nature to be open. Ingenuous is the word for them, I guess." She smiled and turned to the girls: "How long you be in Bangkok, Noi?"

"One maybe two yah," she said eagerly. "Bangkok numbah one. Have too much falang. He numbah one. Have ooooh too much money. Make Noi wewy hoppy."

"Chiang Mai no have too much falang," Dang complained, glancing sidelong at Somsak who intently poured Scotch into his glass. "Have too much Thai man. He numbah ten. Make too much bad Noi and Dang."

"Have you mother and father in Chiang Mai?" Susan asked.

Dang looked downcast. "No have mudah. No have fahdah. Have only Noi."

"My fahdah no like stay home," Noi said. "He go Kolat, wuhk Amelicans. My mudah live Chiang Mai my baby sistah. My fahdah no send money. One month one month one month Noi send mudah fwee tousand baht."

"A hundred and fifty bucks a month," Carl figured. "You sure as hell must screw your little ass off for those horny GIs, honey."

"How long have you been in this game, child?" Jill wondered.

"Game...?" Noi repeated, looking puzzled.

"I mean, how long you be hostess?"

Noi brightened. "Two maybe fwee yah. Same same Dang."

"Regular old pros, aren't they?" said Betty flippantly, trying to catch Ward's eye; but he was still lost in the Brubeck medley.

"How old are you?" Susan asked.

"Me seventeen," said Dang. "Same same Noi."

"A precious age," said Jill softly, running a hand up Noi's thin arm, their brown skins blending.

"Seventeen, my foot!" Betty scoffed. "Twenty-three is more like it. Thai women don't show their age. I've taken bloody old grandmothers to be in their thirties."

"A wonderfully precious age," Jill crooned, her hand now in Noi's shiny black hair where it touched her little round bottom; the girl gazed uncertainly into the dark eyes, and Jill smiled encouragingly. "A beautiful child. She reminds me of someone I knew in Jamaica..."

"Your mother, perhaps?" Betty suggested sourly.

"Mother?" Carl grunted. "Shit. The spook was hatched on a rock from a wet nightmare and raised by vultures."

Ignoring them, Jill devoured Noi with her eyes. "Jill like Noi ooooh too much," she purred.

"You spik Thai?" Noi squeaked.

"*Nid-noi*...a little."

"Me spik Inglish numbah ten."

"It's delightful."

"You like Thailand?"

"Love it."

"You like Thai food?"

"Very much."

"You like Thai guhl?"

"This one, oh, yes..."

Carl howled. "Look who's gettin' this little hooker's GI routine, for fuck's sake!"

Noi buried her face in her hands. "Me solly, Miss Jill," she said bewilderedly. "Me fohget you guhl same same me."

"It's all right, my sweet," Jill soothed, stroking Noi's flowing lock. "Pay no attention to that bloody creep."

"Ask them why they do it for money," Maria demanded.

"Don't be ridiculous," said Jim.

"Why not?"

"It's pointless, that's why."

"But they enchant you, don't they? So ask them, damn it!"

"My dear Maria," said Freddy, as Noi and Dang began to look more and more perplexed. "A proper gentleman would never think of asking a lady why she... Well, why she..."

"Peddles her ass," Carl finished.

Freddy glared at him. "That is not how I was going to put it."

"Ask them if they'd like something to eat," said Wilma. "The poor things must be starved... Frank! Ward! Really, are they in another world over there?"

"Hullo, Wilma," Ward responded, slowly coming round. "What's up, old dear?"

"Your young ladies, for goodness' sake. You neglect them shamefully. Now please see that they get some food. You as well. There's loads on the buffet." And smiling into Dang's appealing young face she asked: "Hungry, my dear?"

She nodded eagerly. "Dang wewy hungwee. Same same Noi." Without further ado she bounced to her feet, grabbed Noi's hand, and pulled her to her feet and to the buffet. Lifting the covers on the tureens and platters, they jabbered excitedly over each discovery, and started to spoon generous portions onto large plates.

"Well," said Wilma, watching with amusement. "Who needs the man what brung you? You could get the girls a drink, Ward. A gin tonic, perhaps?"

"They don't drink," he said, moving off the landing with Frank. "At the Dew Drop they had tea and at the price of tea because they don't cheat. They don't smoke either." He grinned. "They're free of our worst vices."

As Frank changed the record, and Ward filled their glasses at the table, Noi and Dang, chattering away and looking pleased as Punch with their heaped helpings of fish, pilaff and curry and rice, followed Alun into the courtyard and on to her kitchen.

Smiling softly, her knees clasped to her breasts, Jill watched them go, the tip of her tongue playing along her full red lips.

Betty lit another cigarette, inhaled sharply, and relaxed with her drink against an arm of Wilma's chair. "The last we'll see of that pair for a while, I hope," she murmured.

"Now they're with Alun," Maria said bitterly. "And Alun, bless the gossipy little soul, will tell them every darn thing she knows about us, and how we came to be the prime suspects in the murder of her precious mistress."

Chapter Seven

"Maria's right, of course," said Betty. "I'm bloody sure those little whores are getting an earful out there. Thai servants will blab to anybody about anything they see or hear."

"They love to gossip," said Maria simply. "It's Thailand's national pastime. And when you see servants together on their *soi* or in the markets, you can bet they're gabbing about the *farangs* they work for. We're their favourite entertainment." She glanced at Somsak. "And they spy on us for the police."

He smiled. "The police get information from many sources, Miss Maria," he confided, wondering idly to himself how his section could possibly keep a thorough eye on *farangs* without its servant grapevine.

"You should talk about servants spying on us for the police, Maria," said Jim reprovingly.

"I don't know what you mean."

"You know damn well what I mean. You get my girl, Nit, to tell you who phones, who writes, who comes to my house."

"Who you hump," Carl threw in.

"Probably. Does she, Maria?"

"Don't be silly. I don't listen to Nit. Anyway, you make yourself the talk of the neighbourhood by bringing all those little tramps home."

"Do you know," said Ward. "I don't think I have ever heard a *farang* conversation that failed to mention our servants."

"Well, let's face it," said Betty. "They entertain us too. Such eager little ferrets, every last one of them. They sure help us know our neighbours."

"And their most private moments," said Wilma knowingly. "I must tell you a precious story about one of our Saigon wives that Madli heard from Alun. This woman, like other Saigon wives, rarely sees her husband. Can't tear himself away from his Vietnamese girl, I suppose. So she often visits a Danish embassy fellow, a bachelor, next door. His servant told Alun they spend a lot of time in bed, and whenever he gets her excited she shouts 'Oi! Oi! Oi!'. So now..." she chuckled, "...now all the servants around there call her Mrs. Oi. 'There goes Mrs. Oi', they will say to one another when she passes by." And she began to shake with laughter.

"That is precious!" Betty chortled, hugging her knees and rocking gleefully on her bottom. "Who is this Saigon wife, Wilma?"

She caught her breath. "Really, I mustn't say. But once Madli ran into her on their *soi* and without thinking..." She dabbed her eyes with a napkin. "She said, 'Hello, Mrs. Oi'. The poor woman didn't know what to make of it!" And off she went again, sparking a ripple of laughter round the circle.

Though Susan looked pained. "Nothing's sacred, is it?" she sighed.

"Absolutely nothing," Maria sniffed. "You should hear the repulsive way my family's servants talk about *farangs*. It makes me regret that I know Thai."

"Some men would envy Mrs. Oi's Viking lover," said Ward, easing himself to the floor by Susan's end of the sofa, a Scotch and plate of pilaff in hand. "She rewards his passion with cries of joy, a response to lovemaking that's quite beyond certain women. They submit as if it's their duty, then fritter away the heat of the moment. Pick their teeth, perhaps. Or read a script..."

"Paddi...?!" Betty blurted.

"I know what ya' mean," said Carl wisely.

"Do you, Carl? Are you getting into Paddi while I'm up-country on Seato affairs?"

"I'm talkin' about women like that, for fuck's sake."

"Just curious. I sometimes wonder if she's any different with other men. And you didn't answer my question -"

"Hey, buddy boy," Frank cut in. "The music stopped."

"Yes, I know. But long ago, Frank..."

"Well, we'll soon fix that," he said, parking his plate on the buffet and topping his glass on his way to the stereo. "Now let's see, what'll it be?"

"Love's sweet joy is not hard to find," Betty murmured, looking softly on Ward as Frank sifted through the records.

"Don't think we've got that..."

"It's another kind of melodious arrangement she has in mind, Frank," said Wilma, giving Betty's arm a squeeze.

He grinned. "I hear ya', Wilma." Selecting the Beatle's 'Yesterday', he put it on at low volume, and settled on the stair landing once more.

For a minute or so the song's plaintive chords and lyrics silenced the circle, an unusual quiet abruptly shattered when Alun slipped in with more ice-cubes and Betty sprang to her feet. "Tell Alun we can look after ourselves, Wilma. She's heard enough."

"More than enough if you ask me," Wilma allowed as she turned to Alun. "Now listen carefully, my girl. I want you to clear the buffet, put the leftovers in the fridge, then go to your room. You can do the dishes in the morning. You've had a long day and you must be tired."

"*Mai pen lai*, madam! Nemah mine! Me no tied! Can do too much wuhk!"

Wilma shook her head firmly. "You will do no more tonight. It is very late and we will be here for some time. I want you fresh in the morning. Now do as I say."

"Madam..." she began dejectedly.

"Come on, Alun," said Betty, taking her arm and steering her to the buffet. "I'll give you a hand."

"Alun!"

She jumped and froze, fixing an open-mouthed stare on Somsak. He spoke roughly to her in Thai; nodding intensely, she nervously squeaked an answer and quickly began to load dishes onto trays. Again he spoke harshly, this time setting off a whimpering trembling that rattled the china till Betty sharply shushed her to stop.

"Can you be sure, Somsak?" Maria asked.

"I'm positive," he replied calmly.

"Sorry," said Wilma. "I have only taxi Thai and that's abominable."

"It has to do with Madli's murder," Maria explained. "Somsak has made Alun promise not to say a word about that and this gathering to anyone, Thai or *farang*."

"But why did she get so upset?"

"Well, he reminded her of a threat he apparently made when he first questioned her about the circumstances of the murder. If Alun doesn't keep quiet about everything, he will have her banished to her village in the barren North-East. There's nothing there but miserable poverty."

"And he would do it too," said Jim, grinning his appreciation at Somsak. "But Alun would have been in her glory out there with our little friends. She'd have to let them in on a bit of juicy gossip. Ask her in Thai what she said, Maria."

"Jim, really…"

"Come on. Just for fun."

Sighing resignedly, she spoke briefly to Alun, who swiftly brightened and went on at length in high-pitched excitement; Maria looked disgusted. "She told them, and in sickening detail, if you please, how Wilma's French neighbour entertains men in the nude in her swimming pool when her husband is up-country on business."

"Good Lord!" said Wilma, shaking her head in wonder. "And she has been in this house only a day and a half!"

Alun avoided her gaze; head down, she followed Betty out the door with a tray of tureens, grazing Noi and Dang as they came in with empty trays, a bucket of ice cubes, and wide smiles. They dropped the bucket on the floor and began clearing the long table of full ashtrays and empty bottles and plates; when they bent, the tight white sailor pants stretched alarmingly over their firm round bottoms.

Carl licked his lips. "Christ," he breathed. "Look at that, will ya'? I could sure as hell split those pretty cheeks apart about now… But shit, we better tell 'em to blow or every God damn bar in Bangkok will know all about this fuckin' business by tomorrow night."

Jill stirred. "They're harmless," she declared lazily. "They understand only what we spell out clearly and simply. Alun is different. She's been with *farangs* for years. She understands too damn well."

"Yeah," said Frank. "They're okay, no sweat." He dropped the player lid on a spinning Gerry Mulligan disc and chuckled, "I get a bang outa' Dang."

"Your last bang outa' Dang held up the booze," Carl grumbled, and turning to Ward said, "So what's with you and the other chick? You thinkin' of dippin' your wick in her again?"

"Hardly," said Ward, winking at Jill. "I seem to have lost the dear girl."

Leaning sideways in his chair, Carl thrust his heavy freckled face close to Jill, his eyes narrowed. "Toss ya' for her, spook," he challenged.

"Not a chance, pig!" she snarled, pushing him away. "Your brute size would hurt the poor child. Such darling little dolls they are... And lookee here, they got us all tidied up so we can make another mess."

The table now clean and their trays full, Noi and Dang headed for the kitchen, passing Betty as she came in from the courtyard; she jerked her head after them. "They're leaving here, I trust."

"I'm afraid not," Maria said sourly.

Betty plunked herself on her cushion by Wilma and frowned on Ward. "You must be mad," she said angrily.

"Believe me, Betty," he said innocently. "I had nothing whatever to do with it."

"Come off it. Who do you think you're kidding?"

"He's right, Betty," said Wilma. "It was Jill and Frank who felt it wouldn't hurt to let the girls stay, and no one objected. Anyway, my dear, you have no need to worry about Noi."

"Somebody want me?" Noi chirped, hearing her name as she tripped happily into the room with Dang.

"Oh, yes," Jill murmured, holding out her hand. "I want you, pretty baby."

Her lively smile fading, Noi exchanged a puzzled look with Dang, and glanced round as if seeking approval.

"Come to Jill, my darling."

She hesitated a moment longer, eyes blinking, then inched towards the outstretched hand, and taking it, allowed herself to be gently lowered onto the big puffy cushion; their bodies touched.

"Relax," Jill purred, slipping an arm round her. "Enjoy the show."

Rising unsteadily, Carl glared at her. "Fuckin' bitch," he growled, snatching a bottle of Scotch from the table and retreating to the buffet; he leaned against it, scowling over his glass and muttering to himself.

"Dang!" Frank called. "Come to me, baby." Sinking on to the stair landing, he braced his back against the wall and opened his arms and legs, beckoning with his fingers and a wide grin.

Beaming, she squared her thin shoulders and pushed out her small pointed breasts. "Fwank like Dang ooooh too much," she said proudly. "Me pwetty guhl. He numbah one man." Gracefully picking her way up the room to the landing, she sat her tight little bottom between his legs, snuggled against his big chest, and gazed up into his dark eyes. "Dang stay Fwank long long time, hokay?" He enveloped her in his arms and buried his face in her lustrous black hair.

"Very friendly, aren't they?" said Susan, smiling wistfully.

"Revolting!" Maria hissed, glaring at Jim when he laughed.

"They're the first little hostesses I've had here," said Wilma. "I find them rather delightful."

"So did Madli," said Ward. "Their uninhibited sensual dancing excited her. Now and then I brought a couple of the girls over very late for her to dance with. All without a stitch on. Sheer abandon." He took a quick nip. "Incredible nights, they were."

"I had no idea," Wilma said weakly. "Did you, Jill?"

"Madli and I had our own thing," she murmured, whirling scornfully on Jim and Carl when they exchanged knowing winks and grins. "You studs probably had something to do with that whip under her bed!"

"My goodness!" said Wilma.

"Come on, Wilma," Jill sighed. "Nothing our Madli did surprised or shocked any more."

"Well, I knew her in different moods too, of course. Now that I think of it, I did see something of the Madli that Ward described when we dropped in for a cold beer at that GI hang-out, the Villa Club. It was always her idea, and usually at night when the place was packed with our young soldiers and their Thai girls. They liked to invite us to sit at their tables for the pleasure of talking with *farang* women for a change. A rather homesick pleasure, I felt. They regaled us with stories of family and sweethearts back home, and descriptions of their duties in Vietnam or at our bases in Thailand. Our boys liked Madli. She listened sympathetically. And she applauded their wild dancing. I'm sure the young devils spurred their girls on to more feverish gyrations for our benefit. Yes, and quite often Madli would join couples on the floor and simply let herself go. A revelation to me, I must say. She seemed carried away."

"Perhaps Noi and Dang would give us a wild and wicked display," Betty suggested playfully.

"Not tonight, surely," said Susan hastily. "I thought..."

Suddenly a rumbling snore erupted from the Reverend Ralph. He slumped in his chair, chins on his chest, paunch in his lap, and wisps of damp grey hair stuck to his brow; drool from his wheezing lips stained his old school tie, a sock soaked up drops of gin from the tilted glass in his right hand, and his left hand, resting on his right forearm, seemed to point accusingly at Freddy.

"I was quietly humming him a little song," he said defensively. "A jolly quietly little song when suddenly..." he pointed his gin bottle, "...he went like this."

"What an edifying sight," said Betty.

"I better take him home," said Beatrice, standing and wringing her hands.

"Sit down, Beatrice," Paul told her sternly; Tim leaned drowsily against his father's left leg and Meg rested an arm on his right knee, her blank gaze on Beatrice now.

"But it's nearly midnight," she said anxiously. "And Ralph is not a young man. His back -" She caught herself, suddenly flustered.

"What's wrong with his back?" Paul asked brusquely.

"It's just that... Well... He tires so easily."

"So what? He's asleep."

"Not to worry, old girl," Freddy assured her. "I have known chaps to sleep much better like this..." his bottle swung towards the Reverend, "...than in a feather bed." The bottle swung back in an arch and landed neck down in his glass. The Reverend lapsed into a light wheeze which fluttered his soggy lips.

"Please let me take him home," Beatrice begged.

"Sit down," Paul ordered, eyeing her severely till she meekly complied, clasping her hands in her lap and casting a worried look at her husband. "You seem to forget..." He took in the others: "You all seem to forget we are trying to find out which one of you murdered my wife."

"That's not what I'm trying to do," Jill yawned, pressing Noi's sleepy head to her breast.

"Nor I," Susan sighed.

"But Paul," said Beatrice fearfully. "Surely you don't suspect Ralph and me...?"

"I suspect every last one of you," he replied coldly.

"Really, Paul," said Wilma. "You can be quite disagreeable in your semi-sober state. I do wish you would drink up and -"

"Let's get on with it!" he insisted angrily.

"I'm with you, old man!" Freddy seconded cheerfully with a wave of his bottle.

"I think I'd rather play dirty word scrabble," said Ward.

"You *what?*" said Betty, staring at him in disbelief. "This was your idea, for God's sake. You were so bloody sure we would all feel better if we could show Somsak, right here and now, that Madli could not have been killed by one of us. Let's bare our souls and our alibis to try to clear ourselves of suspicion, you said. Now you want to back out. Why?"

"Afraid?" Jill taunted.

"Yes. But not for the reason you might suspect. I'm thinking of what I told you about Madli dancing starkers with bar girls, and wondering what other tales could..." He turned to Paul. "It might be wiser to let Somsak investigate your wife's murder without our questionable help."

"Wiser and kinder," said Susan, glancing at Meg.

"I know what you're saying, Ward," Paul conceded restlessly. "But the murder solution must be found quickly or it may soon be out of reach, and it's better to follow your idea, haphazard though it sounds, than have Somsak plod through a dozen interrogations and probes that could be baffled. At least the pursuit of the murderer begins with an advantage. The keys confine it to this room."

"The keys?" Ward echoed.

"Ah, we forget," said Betty. "You and Frank were rounding up booze and bar girls when Paul dropped that wee bombshell."

"And he has a theory to go with it," said Jim. "He claims a *kamoy* didn't do it because Alun locked the house tight as a drum after Madli went to bed, and next morning there was not a sign of a break in. And he claims Madli didn't answer the door after Alun was in her outside room because Alun would've heard the knocker or the bell and the greetings. It seems she was awake till nearly three and the police doctor put Madli's death at around two-thirty. No sir. Paul is dead certain that somebody with a key sneaked into the house and shot Madli with a pistol he gave her in Saigon. It's the same calibre as the bullet they found in her body, and it's gone."

"Somebody with a key," Ward mused.

"Yeah," said Carl. "Somehow he found out that Madli gave a key to her house to everybody here except Maria, and what the hell, she could lift Jim's key any fuckin' time she -"

"But I didn't!" she cried, looking anxiously to Jim.

"Nobody said you did," he told her wearily. "Anyway, Ward, now you know why Paul invited only us to Madli's funeral and to Wilma's afterward."

"So he could set us up for this phoney hunt for her killer, for fuck's sake," Carl griped; and glancing from Ward to Frank said, "You guys got a key, right?"

"Right," said Ward, catching Frank's stony nod. "And Alun had her key, of course. As I remember she kept it on a string round her neck."

"She was entertaining some clown in her room at the time Madli died," Jill said. "It must have been a riot. She didn't even hear the shot... Hey. Could the shot be heard out there, Somsak?"

"Very unlikely," he answered firmly. "The house was closed. So was Mrs. Madli's room and it's on the other side. As well, the sound could have been muffled by the way the pistol was held. It was quite close. There were powder marks round the wound. I would think the shot could have been heard a bit upstairs. But the children's doors were closed, and they slept."

"Madli too?" Jim wondered.

"Not by the look on her face," said Somsak.

"She saw death coming," Jill whispered.

"The poor dear soul," Wilma mourned.

"I guess she knew her executioner," Carl said matter-of-factly.

"It was one of her lovers," Maria huffed. "It must have been. She had nothing on."

"The way she always slept," said Ward. "I would say it was someone who knew where she kept that pistol. I did. Who else...?"

"Don't answer that," said Betty smartly. "A moment ago he wanted us to stop meddling in the investigation. Now he's doing it again."

"Well," he said thoughtfully. "The keys do seem to narrow everything down to us."

"Damn right they do!" Freddy cried triumphantly, his bottle pointing in all directions. "And even old Somsak knew nothing about the keys. Nor the pistol. Bully for you, Paul, old man!"

"Surely Madli didn't tell you about the keys, Paul," said Ward.

He shook his head, slowly, deliberately.

"Alun must have told him," Wilma said. "My God. She better keep her little nose out of things round here."

"Alun was not aware that you all had a key," Paul said, placing his hand on Meg's shoulder. She gazed calmly at her mother's friends and lovers.

They strained to hear her small voice: "I told Daddy about the keys and everything."

Chapter Eight

Meg's sudden admission made the mystery of her mother's murder still more puzzling to Somsak. It meant that she had always known just who had a key to the house, and that it was she who found the little pistol was missing. Yet for some reason Meg had given this crucial information only to her father, and for some reason Paul had kept it from him till he told the murder suspects. But why? Was Paul trying to trap Madli's killer on his own out of vengeance? And was he afraid that if his selected guests got wind of his evidence before her funeral they might tumble to his purpose, and guilty or not, keep clear of this gathering for fear of what it might reveal? Well, what else...? Somsak sighed inwardly, though not so much for the answers that eluded him as for the ridicule he expected from Jill over Meg's few telling words. Instead, they brought an angry outburst from Wilma.

"You're to blame, Paul. Our dear Madli would be alive, and Meg would have been spared all this, if you had listened to me and sent your family away from Southeast Asia when American dependants had to leave Vietnam in 'sixty-five!"

"That's cruel and unfair!" he protested hotly. "Madli insisted on being close by in Bangkok so the children could see their father now and then. Many wives moved here from Vietnam for the same reason."

"The poor misguided fools," said Jill. "All these years a Saigon wife, a fate far worse than death."

"Ah, but lest we forget," said Betty. "They also serve who simply go to pieces in Bangkok while their men carry on with the war in Vietnam."

Carl chuckled, "Carry on with Vietnamese broads is more like it. When old LBJ said clear the decks and press on with the war, the guys I knew with wives or families in 'Nam were fuckin' glad to be rid of 'em so they could press on with all that Saigon screwin'."

"Not all our men were so obscene," Wilma said. "Some were like my Dick, I'm sure. He would much rather I stayed with him in Saigon, but wives and children were in the way. Men can't concentrate on war if they must worry about the safety of loved ones. And it is quite dangerous there."

"It is dangerous here as well," said Paul, "as you all are now aware."

"It's unfortunate that you were not aware before now, Paul. You might have put your foot down and made Madli wait out this awful war in London as I suggested. It was your home for years. You had many friends there. I could never understand why she -"

"She could not be persuaded. I tried. I knew it would be best for her and the children. And I knew she loved London. I did too."

"And I, Paul," said Freddy, smiling soulfully over his glass.

Betty grimaced. "I was born there and I loathe the place. Dirty old buildings, buses and tubes. Rude shop girls, snooty neighbours, grimy skinheads, phoney toffs and models, relentless rain, wintry summers. No thanks."

Ward laughed. "Laying it on a bit thick, aren't you, Betty?"

"A tiny bit, perhaps," she allowed. "I just fail to see why anyone is enamoured of London."

"Yet many are," said Susan. "You met Madli there, didn't you, Paul?"

"Not in London," he replied, smiling softly on Meg. "Her mother and I met in Paris."

"In a bar I bet," said Jill, gently moving the sleeping Noi from her breast to her lap.

"I had a day in Paris on my way back from the States last summer," Jim said. "I didn't see much."

"I'm not surprised," Maria sniffed. "You probably spent the whole time in bed with some French tramp."

"It was 1949," said Paul, gazing beyond them. "I was with the United States Information Service at our London embassy. Occasionally I went to Paris for a weekend, and -"

"For the whores, right?" said Carl. "I hear the Paris pros are pretty fuckin' good."

"...and one Sunday, as I stood on the Arc de Triomphe and marvelled at those grand boulevards that run from its broad circle like spokes of a huge wheel, I was approached by a young woman in a fitted coat of orange and green tweed that I remember vividly..."

"Guess who?" Jill quipped.

"She asked me in halting French to identify a building on a distant hill. It was the Sacre Coeur. For some reason I told her in English. She responded in English, which was far better than her French. She said I sounded like an American. I admitted I was indeed a Yank. She smiled..." He paused, his eyes reflecting a kind of aching. "Do you know, when we said goodbye to Madli a few hours ago, she looked as she did then. Long and flowing yellow hair, exquisite features, a clear complexion. On that fresh spring day a touch of roses was in her cheeks, and her eyes, an extraordinary blue, seemed to sparkle with life. Her lips..." He sighed. "Oh, yes, when she smiled I was a goner. Soon we were sitting at a sidewalk cafe on the Champs Elysées, drinking wine, talking, laughing, remarking on the passing parade. An exhilarating moment, and a fateful one. I was thirty, single, and fancy-free. She was quite a bit younger, it turned out. And unattached."

"Ah, Paris," Wilma sighed. "It belongs to the young and fancy-free."

He nodded. "So we like to think... Well, as it happened, she too worked in London and had come to Paris alone for the weekend, and for the first time. I suggested we see a bit of the city and go back together. She cheerfully agreed and off we went. First to the left bank for a delightful stroll by the Seine and a browse through its many bookstalls in St. Germain-des-Prés. Then a long walk through a tangle of interesting streets to Monmartre where we had dinner among the entertaining low-life on Avenue Clichy. We made the last boat-train to Calais by the skin of our teeth. The ferry trip to Dover was spent on deck in the moonlight, and in that charming accent she never quite lost, Madli began to talk about herself. Happily when she recalled her childhood before the war, painfully when she came to the tragic blows the war dealt her...."

"She was Estonian, an only child. The family lived on her maternal grandfather's farm near the Baltic Sea. Her mother helped run it and her father taught physics at a university. He and Madli were devoted to one another. Together they poured over books, wandered the countryside and trails by the sea, and lost themselves in fairy tales from his childhood. In the war, the German occupation was very harsh. The Russian advance near the end of it was a nightmare. During a battle near the farm a stray shell killed her grandfather. Her father disappeared in the confusion of the fighting. Madli and her mother, forced to give him up for dead, fled south. A few miles down the road they were caught by a Russian tank crew..."

Looking troubled, he turned to Meg; she took his hand, nodded slightly, and he went back to the others. "My memories and knowledge of Madli are special and private. It never seemed right to confide in anyone. Yet if I can tell you anything that will help loosen a few -"

"The Russian tank crew, for fuck's sake," Carl pressed.

"They brutally beat and raped Madli and her mother. Hours later she came to in a ditch beside her mother's lifeless body. She was badly injured and in dreadful pain and fear. But somehow, moving mostly at night and hiding by day in deserted farm houses and bombed-out buildings, and living on scraps of food she found here and there, she made her way through the Russian and German lines to the British positions in the west. She had lost track of the days, and all sense of time. Finally, weak and exhausted from hunger and injury, she collapsed by a roadside. Army medics found her, and for a while she was aware of their kindness and care. Then she knew nothing more till the day she began to notice her surroundings in a ward of Middlesex Hospital in London.

"She had been sent there for intensive care, her condition was that critical. Once she was well enough to leave, the hospital was reluctant to let her go. They were concerned for her welfare. She was asked to stay as a nurse's aide and live in their dormitory, and she gratefully agreed. She was a clerk in charge of patient's records when our paths crossed..." He drank slowly, his gaze drifting past them.

Maria shuddered. "Imagine telling someone you just met that a bunch of Russian soldiers raped you and murdered your mother. Surely something so distressing should be kept to yourself."

"In different circumstances maybe," said Ward. "But a romance was brewing, and perhaps Madli, for Paul's sake, wanted him to know of her dreadful experience before he plunged ahead. Lesser men might have backed off."

"She was only a child when it happened," Beatrice murmured.

"Filthy bloody Russians!" Freddy blustered.

"Come off it," Jill scoffed. "Soldiers everywhere do that. Women are spoils of war in their warped minds. Help yourself." She closed her arm round Noi. "No woman is safe from the military."

Frank grunted and shifted his rump on the landing, rousing a sleepy whimper from the girl in his arms.

"What must you have felt, Paul?" Susan wondered.

He frowned. "Anger and sadness. I could see her crumpled by that roadside as the British medics found her. Battered, bruised and exhausted, her long yellow hair matted with grime. It was enough to make you weep. I took her in my arms and she clung to me tearfully. She said she was sorry to burden me with her frightful experience, but if we continued, it would help me to understand certain feelings that sometimes possessed her. And God knows I wanted us to continue. I loved her, dammit. It came over me quite rapidly in those hours after we met on the Arc de Triomphe. I told her this. She smiled through her tears and said that such confessions under stress are often regretted. I guaranteed I'd never regret mine. And I didn't... Not once after that did Madli mention her torture by Russian soldiers. Neither did I till now..."

"Did you have to tell us?" Maria griped. "It has no bearing -"

"Oh yes it has," Betty said quickly. "Madli is the immortal subject of this jolly gathering when it's not side-tracked by drunks, servants or bar girls. Anything about her is relevant."

"I'll buy that," said Jim. "You never know..."

"Poor Madli," Wilma grieved. "Such an awful thing to have in one's memory. But Paul, the feelings she was anxious for you to understand. When did they appear?"

"Eventually," he said, glancing at Meg. "Anyway, before our train from Dover arrived at Victoria, Madli had become cheerful and amusing once more. We took a cab to her small flat near the East End hospital where she worked. She made coffee and we chatted. I didn't make any passes. I was too chastened by her disturbing story. Besides, she soon packed me off to my Bloomsbury apartment. Our long day had tired her. She couldn't keep her eyes open. When we embraced and kissed good night, she urged me to come the next evening. I didn't need urging. I began to see her most evenings and weekends. We did West End shows, galleries, museums, shopping in Harrods, pub dinners. We wandered afield to grand castles, stately homes and Kentish gardens, lingering over village teas and picnics in meadows..."

He smiled faintly. "It was heaven to be with her. We talked about our work, our colleagues, our love of London, our tastes in books, music, theatre, food, anything. Or silently walked arm in arm, her closeness and scent playing merry hell with my senses..." He sighed deeply. "I wanted her. Christ how I wanted her. But when I became amorous she put me off, gently yet firmly. I was desperate, and it must have showed. One night I sensed her giving in. I pressed, and she broke away, curling up in tears and whimpering achingly. The effect of her cruel beating and rape, of course, and the certain feelings I'd been told to expect. It was heartbreaking. I held her and told her I loved her. I could wait. I understood..."

"No way," Jill sneered. "You think she kept her legs crossed out of fear. I think she spurned your attempt to get into her with a bit of sham because she couldn't bear to have men touch her. At that time men repelled her. All men. I understand too well."

"You understand bugger all!" he retorted. "Madli's responses were from the heart. It was not her nature to be phoney. And men didn't repel her at that time. She liked men. Instinctively."

"And they liked her, no doubt," Wilma put in before Jill could reply.

"Always. Madli was a desirable young woman. She had beauty, grace, charm, sympathy, intelligence. Our embassy crowd adored her. She seemed to blossom when we got out and about, displaying a lively wit, a gay sense of fun, a boundless imagination, and a keen interest in the jobs and opinions of others. It was her doing that made us popular guests at receptions, dinners, theatre parties and weekend retreats in the country. We were constantly on the go, it seemed. A wonderful -"

"Momento," said Betty. "Was no one curious about her origins and past? I would be."

"Well, London had many refugees from behind the Iron Curtain. Madli knew quite a few, some with tragic stories that got around one way or another. Naturally, friends were curious about Madli's story too, but she wasn't grilled. They accepted what little she told them. She was simply known as that lovely Estonian with the delightful accent, presence and manners. I was envied no end...

"It was a wonderful year, though we lived apart and her fear of physical love kept me as chaste as a monk. I wanted us to get married. Whenever I pursued it, she asked me to be patient. She wasn't ready. At times I despaired that she ever would be, but I was in for a surprise. In Paris on the anniversary of our meeting, as we stood hand in hand on the Arc de Triomphe where it began, she suddenly pressed close and said we belonged together, so we should be man and wife. I think I whooped for joy. The very next week we tied the knot at the register office in Chelsea."

Betty groaned. "Why do lovers have to spoil everything by getting married?"

"Rubbish," said Maria, getting to her feet and stepping over Ward's legs to reach a case of liquor by the end of the table. "Marriage makes everything much better."

"Look out, Jim," Carl warned, watching her open a bottle of Scotch and start freshening glasses. "This one has her fuckin' hooks out."

Jim grinned at her, and Maria shot both a withering look. "Don't condemn marriage because some people make a mess of it. I'm sure it can be made quite idyllic."

"If you find a perfect mate, perhaps," said Betty. "And there's a fat chance of that."

"Easy to choose an imperfect mate when you're head over heels in love," Wilma said, handing her glass to Maria. "Mine is gin, dear. A little tonic and ice will do. And take Frank a Scotch so he'll not have to get up and waken his darling Dang."

"The idyllic marriage," Ward pondered. "I'm afraid it's an illusion with me. Our glow started to fade as Paddi unpacked from our honeymoon... And you, Paul. Did your wedding vows change anything?"

"No, not really. The pleasure of being with Madli didn't fade. Mind you, there were tense moments when we finally loved as man and wife. It was quite a while before she could relax, and years before she would even think of having a child. Then at last..." He looked tenderly at his daughter, "at last she agreed and along came Meg."

"You found the knack, old man!" Freddy cried, banging his empty bottle on the arm of his chair.

"Good God!" said Betty. "He's done it again. How can one human being go through a whole bottle of gin in a couple of hours?"

"Freddy tries harder," Jill cracked.

"No wonder the Seato alliance is a big joke in Moscow, Peking and Hanoi with boozers like him in charge."

Freddy glared at her. "You don't like Australians, do you, Miss Witty Betty?"

"Not in particular."

"And why not, may I ask?"

"Because you're a lot of boorish barbarians."

He ground his teeth. "Whorish librarians indeed! Bloody Pommy. One thing wrong with London, Paul. It's full of bloody Pommies!"

"We lived outside London in Sunbury-on-Thames," he said absently, intent on freshening his glass.

"Dreary little village," Betty sniped. "The river's the only attraction."

"We rented a lovely restored rectory on the river, and there were many pleasant walks round about. Madli quit her hospital job to run the house. She enjoyed it. Her artistic flair brightened our rooms with flowers, furnishings, paintings and colours. She had a green thumb. Her roses were the envy of the village. And she was a marvellous hostess. Our dinners were memorable for her dishes and the way she drew people out to stimulate the table talk. We entertained a lot in those days. Friends in diplomacy, the military, the theatre, our own community, the Middlesex hospital, and the eastern European émigré crowd." He shook his head reflectively. "Good times they were. Loving, cheerful, busy -"

"Boozy," Jill threw in.

"Somewhat."

"Somewhat?" she mocked. "A hell of a lot more than somewhat from all I've seen and heard. When I first met you here in Bangkok you were soaked in whisky. And your wife's indifference to boot. Yet you hung in. Didn't you get the message?"

He gulped his drink and stared at her. "Message?" he queried. "The order to cut and run, is that what you mean? Civilised couples don't forsake one another if the magic that brought them together wears out for some reason."

"Bullshit. Civilised couples have killed one another, and for endless reasons, once that magic dies. You were insanely jealous because she revelled in the wild oats she was able to sow at last. And there was only one way to stop it. You murdered her!"

"That's utter nonsense!" he spluttered. "I loved her. I would never think of harming her. What's more, I was in Saigon when she was murdered."

She shrugged. "So what? You can hire a killer in Bangkok for as little as twenty-five dollars. I can find you one right now in Pratunam Market. You were here a few weeks ago. You could have paid a hit man to kill Madli, given him your key to the house, and told him where to find her pistol to do the job."

"Hang on," said Ward. "Anyone with a key could have had Madli killed that way. But you'd risk blackmail, and having your throat cut if you didn't pay up."

"Paul was safe in Saigon, wasn't he?" she said pointedly. "Yet he could have her blood on his hands. How say you, Somsak?"

"It's not possible," said Susan quickly. "Surely Paul would not gather us here as the prime suspects if he had -"

"Why not? It could be a charade to put himself above suspicion. Has anyone thought of that? Come on, Somsak. On with the cuffs."

"Miss Jill," he said patiently. "First we must find out if -"

"I can save you the trouble, Somsak," said Paul. "I don't have a key to that house. I was never given one."

There were surprised looks, and Betty giggled, "How droll. Everyone but the husband gets a key to his wife's house."

"You can have my key, Paul," Freddy offered. "I shan't be needing it any longer."

"No key to your family's home?" Wilma stressed. "Why not, for heaven's sake?"

"No need. I could never stay long. A weekend at most. My home is a small suite in the Caravelle Hotel in Saigon. The Bangkok house was Madli's. I paid the bills and flew in every month or so to see the children."

"The children," Jill sneered. "If they weren't so bloody obvious I would never believe that Madli was a mother. It didn't suit her at all as far as I'm concerned."

"She was a good mother," said Meg suddenly, sitting up on her cushion, her empty gaze on the circle. "She loved Tim and me. She took good care of us. She did many things with us. Our years in England were wonderful because of Mother. She took me to school and fetched me when it was out. We went on long walks and shopped in the high street and sometimes met Daddy's train from London. She said our Tim looked like Daddy, and one day I would look like her. She -"

"Enough!" Jill cried, clapping her hands over her ears. "No more of this shit, dammit!"

"Jill!" Susan protested. "Meg's remembering her mother."

"She's rambling on and on like her bloody father! A lot of crap about somebody I don't know and don't want to know!"

"Cool it," said Jim. "She's just a kid."

"Then send them to bed! What the hell are they doing up at this hour anyway?!"

"Their father wants it," Beatrice said quietly.

Jill humphed and nervously lit a cigarette, softly lulling Noi when the girl began to stir from her outburst.

"I'm sorry, Meg dear," said Wilma. "We're all a bit upset."

"It's all right, Aunt Wilma."

"Your mother loved you very much. She told me so, but I could see."

"Yes. We had special moments, Mother and I. She liked to sit at her dressing-table while I brushed her hair. She kept it long and natural. When she played with Tim in the garden it would fall across her face. She'd laugh and tell us how it would do that when she ran before the wind on the cliffs by the Baltic Sea. She told us fairy stories her father had told her as a child. They had a secret place of happiness in a forest glade by the sea, and one day she would take me there." She looked away, her small voice a whisper. "Sometimes when I brushed her hair I could see in the mirror that she was crying. No sound. Just tears. I never asked why. She's remembering, I felt. She would hold me close and talk very fast in Estonian like she did when excited or angry. Nobody understood. Not even Daddy..." Again she leaned on her father's knee, her cheek on her hand, her eyes shadowed.

"My dear Meg," he sighed. "There's a great deal I don't understand."

"Don't fret, old chap," said Freddy. "Only Estonians can fathom it when someone carries on like that in Estonian. It's a most peculiar lingo, you know."

"Peculiar is the word for Madli's behaviour as well," Maria sniffed. "Her odd choice of lovers for instance. And the brazen way she carried on with them. Did you suspect her of being unfaithful when you lived in England, Paul?"

"Not for a moment. Madli attracted men, of course. Her certain glow had them hovering at affairs we attended. Especially a French military attaché and a Swedish journalist. I was curious, and after one party where the Frenchman seemed to pay her a lot of attention, I asked offhand what she thought of him. She sensed a concern. It amused her. She teased me over the evils of suspicion and jealousy. She easily set my mind at rest, as she did when I worried about her coming home late from a day in the city. She liked to walk London, she'd explain. I could appreciate that. So did I. And I loved her, don't forget. My doubts never lasted long."

"You're a rare one then," said Betty. "I bet most men with beautiful wives never shake their doubts once the wolves pick up her scent. Other wives and mistresses might fear or envy her, and she could have trouble making women friends. Did Madli have any back there?"

"Several. The wives or ladies of my embassy colleagues mostly. A young Polish woman at Middlesex Hospital, a former refugee like herself, was her only close friend."

"Very close," Jill murmured. "Madli told me about her."

"A loving family, good friends, a safe job, a pleasant life," Susan recited thoughtfully. "You were well off, Paul. Yet you came to this part of the world at its most perilous time. What were you thinking of?"

"My career. I asked to go to Vietnam. Madli encouraged me. She saw it as a priceless experience for all of us. I saw a chance to get ahead as well. I did in time. Today I run the US Information Service in Saigon. Anyway, we arrived in 'sixty-three, Diem's fatal year. A few hundred American military specialists were openly training and advising his forces, or secretly leading strikes against the North's supply lines next door in Laos and Cambodia. But we weren't getting anywhere. Charley got stronger and bolder. Dozens of our people were killed. It was a mess. Critics at home began hammering Washington over Diem's tyranny and failures. After he was murdered in that CIA-planned coup by Big Min, they were onto us for not making headway in spite of the vast amounts of money, arms and troops lavished on the war. Yet our top brass claim we're winning. Thousands of our young men are being shipped home in bodybags yet the deception goes on. And I can see it becoming even bloodier if we - "

Catching himself, he glanced around warily. "I won't agonise over Vietnam. There's enough of that going on in the world. Tonight we have a crime of a different sort on our conscience. But I'll give Saigon its due. It reeks of corruption, but it appeals. Madli and I were taken by its neat colonial layout and relics, by its friendly people and ancient customs. And my generous government salary and full living allowance put us on Easy Street. We could afford the exorbitant rent of a lovely old French house, rich oriental furnishings, every modern convenience, in a quiet and shady suburb. Servants were plentiful and cheap, so we had a cook, housemaid, gardener-chauffeur, and a nursemaid for little Tim. We sent Meg to a fine French school, joined a country club for the first time, and shopped at our huge PX in Saigon for every comfort and luxury of home at Stateside prices. We had always lived well. But nothing like this..."

"The high life at Uncle Sam's expense," Betty said simply. "This war is a godsend to some of you Yanks."

"It wasn't all for the best. One fateful change was in my work. I had to shepherd news people and visiting bigwigs round the country. I might be gone for days. Madli was alone a great deal. She had time on her hands..." He paused, toying with his glass, nipping the Scotch. "I have no earthly reason to think she might have betrayed me in England," he continued slowly. "We were very close. We had a good life. She adored her children and took pride in her home. She appeared content. And I'm damn sure we would have gone on as we were but for another fateful change in our lives. Many of the people we mixed with in our position were appallingly different from our old crowd in London. Gross, cynical, grasping, uncaring, immoral. The war's walking wounded, and they infected others. I believe the ruination that led to Madli's murder began when she was introduced to their dangerous debauchery by one of our new friends..."

He looked intently down the room, his eyes flashing fire.

"Our dear Wilma!"

Chapter Nine

Ward sank back against the sofa with his glass and watched with amusement as Wilma fumbled with a cigarette and lighter. "Did Madli fall or was she pushed?" he wondered slyly. "That seems to be the question."

"She was pushed," Paul insisted. "Wilma led her into the worst crowd and the most depraved scenes."

The cigarette going at last, she furiously puffed up a cloud of smoke. "I did nothing of the sort," she said indignantly. "I am not my sister's keeper, for heaven's sake. Madli was a friend, a very dear friend. I like to have friends around me. I don't mind how they drink..." - she glanced at Freddy, scowling at his empty bottle, and the Reverend Ralph, wheezing in his sleep on the chair beside him; then smiled faintly at Frank, cradling a drowsy Dang in his arms on the stair landing - "...or how they love. Their behaviour can be outrageous for all I care. But they must answer for it. I can't be blamed for the harm they might do to themselves."

"Maybe not," Jill teased. "But what other innocent lambs have you led astray, Wilma?"

"This one!" Betty squealed. "And I loved it!"

"Shit," Carl grunted. "The only innocent lambs round here are these little Thai whores."

"That's only your mindless opinion, I would hope," Maria hissed, jostling Jim when he laughed.

"Madli certainly wasn't mindless, Paul," said Susan. "Surely she could have avoided the seamy side of Saigon society...?"

"Not easily. It's pervasive."

"Yet you were there to -"

"But rarely. As I told you, my job took me away from Saigon for days at a time. Madli had the children, of course, but she was often alone, and typically restless for something to do. She liked the Vietnamese and wanted to know more about them, but Wilma diverted her to the foreign crowd with its endless carousing and shabby affairs. It was alien to everything we had known in England."

"Then you were looking through rose-coloured glasses, Paul," said Wilma impatiently. "I'll wager that London's embassy scene and its hangers-on are little different from others. Only the cast changes, as Dick and I found in fifteen years with our diplomatic missions in Europe. And when he took over American aid in Vietnam in 'sixty-two, our social world was again a familiar mix. Our own and other embassy people, military officers, journalists, expatriate teachers and businessmen, and builders, suppliers and salesmen trying to wheedle fat contracts with Uncle Sam. Quite a rabble they were at times, I must admit. And some were on the make, certainly. Boozy wingdings and one-night stands were their idea of a good time. But it's like that back home, isn't it? In the country clubs, for instance?"

"Don't be ridiculous," he derided. "No other place can match the loose living by our people in Saigon and Bangkok, for God's sake."

"Well, you may be right," she conceded reluctantly, stubbing her cigarette in an ashtray. "But the war has made people reckless, whether they're in the thick of it or on the fringe. We are all at loose ends and far from home. There are so many uncertainties. It's not surprising to see so much drinking and sleeping around."

"There's something else," said Susan thoughtfully. "Something about Bangkok that makes *farangs* behave that way."

"Damn right there is," said Jill, caressing the bare tummy of her sleeping beauty and smiling softly to herself. "It's something warm, cloying and sensual in the very air we breathe, and it makes you weak with longing for every lustful pleasure."

"You got it, spook!" Carl boomed. "Last month our chief honcho flew in from the States for the first time, so I took him round the Patpong bars and Petchburri massage joints to get him laid. But shit, he smelt it everywhere. It went to his head. He was a walkin' hard-on and clear out of whack in a week. The day he flew out he asked if all we did here was screw. I said hell yes, Bangkok's the screwin' capital of the whole fuckin' world!"

He chuckled as Jim roared and Maria fumed, "Must you laugh at him? He's disgusting!"

"But dead on," Jim countered soberly. "What do you think keeps me here? The God damn temples?!"

"Bangkok and Saigon," Ward mused. "The Sodom and Gomorrah of the Far East, it seems."

"Well put," said Betty. "And Lot's wife is now the Saigon wife, a pillar of lonely despair as she looks back and wonders if her man is in the clutches of a Vietnamese tart. None can be sure. A Seattle girl I met at Pattaya flew home in tears last month. She thought her marriage was solid as a rock, even as a Saigon wife. Then she caught her husband, on one of his rare trips to Bangkok to visit her in exile, buying gifts for his sweetie in Saigon. The rat."

"Yet another broken heart," Susan sighed. "This must be a graveyard of Western marriages."

"Mine is buried here," said Paul. "And my wife. But that wasn't the woman I brought to Saigon." He glared accusingly over his glass at Wilma.

"Don't look at me like that, Paul," she said uneasily. "I don't deserve it, really. My intentions towards your wife were not evil. On the contrary -"

"If only she hadn't met you."

"We were bound to meet. I headed the American Women's Club. I was expected to take newcomers under my wing. We liked one another right away, and Madli seemed to like what we did. Our luncheons, coffee klatch, parties for American children, charity bazaars for Vietnamese orphans, tea with Madame Nu, Diem's charming sister-in-law, and garden parties with their silly competitions for the zaniest hat or costume that are so typically American. I did that sort of thing for years. It's required if you're embassy."

"Then thank God I'm not," said Betty. "Anyway, I'd never get on with the bloody bureaucrats."

"Bigots, all of them," Jill declared. "Look what happened when Lev, that Soviet press attaché who Betty brought round, started teaching some of us Russian. Right away the US. embassy made the Americans in the class pull out. Somebody must've put a bug in their ear..."

"Madli warned us that might happen," Jim recalled. "She'd have nothing to do with Lev's lessons."

"...and when Lev put his little daughter in a ballet school run by Americans, his embassy ordered him to take her out. Can you imagine anything more stupid?"

"There's more to that than meets the eye," Ward maintained. "The American and Soviet missions in Bangkok and Vientiane, as our black humour would have it, run so many spies they're tripping over one another. Funny, perhaps, but not to the big powers. Southeast Asia is in delicate balance, and both try to tip it their way. They're afraid if their people get chummy with the other side they might let slip some valuable information, or be bribed into selling it. A game of nerves and embassy wallahs are not be envied, even if they have dear and dutiful wives like Wilma."

"Well," Maria humphed. "I can't picture Madli of all people as a dutiful embassy wife."

"She was in Saigon," said Wilma. "But we swore off all that nonsense when we moved to Bangkok. We were angry with President Johnson for having us banished from Vietnam. Mind you, the wife of our ambassador to Saigon was sent to safety here as well, and she tried to keep us at it. But we escaped." She smiled at those around her. "And found new friends, new adventures -"

"New rounds of wild and dangerous parties," Paul put in bitterly. "They perverted Madli in Saigon and you know it."

"Really, Paul," she sighed. "I recall very few parties you'd call wild and dangerous. Unavoidable, many of them. We all had to see and be seen. Dick and I introduced you and Madli to Saigon's cocktail circuit, if you remember. Then it was a nine-to-five war." She winced humorously. "My God. When I think of it. We worked on the war for a few hours, then everybody headed for the beaches, the tennis courts and swimming pools, the country club and sports club, the receptions and house parties. I mean everybody. The crooked little generals and colonels in Vietnam, like those in Laos and Thailand, think they serve their country by drinking themselves blotto at our parties and happy hours." She glanced apologetically at Freddy and Ward. "So do many Seato people. I'm afraid the battle against communist rebellions in Southeast Asia is in some pretty shaky hands."

"I agree," said Ward easily, springing to his feet to fix her a gin and tonic. "I'm just thankful that Seato has kept out of the shooting war. Our strange assortment of allies might pop away at each other in utter confusion."

"Well, I for one am utterly confused," said Freddy, peering in Paul's direction. "I say, old man. What's all this I hear? Are you now looking for a jolly wild party instead of the swine who popped off your dear sweet wife?"

"I'm confirming my belief that Wilma helped her downfall in Saigon," he replied irritably.

"No you're not," she retorted sharply. "You have absolutely no grounds for blaming me."

"Indeed I have. You were always together. You had been around and you led her on, exposing her to amoral rot till she behaved that way. Yet all you do -"

"Why are you doing this?"

"All you do is plaster it over with a lot of nonsense about benevolent tea parties and excuses for dissipation. Anybody can see through it, for Christ's sake."

She held his angry glare, sipping her drink, thinking; then said, resignedly, "You've been hurt enough, Paul. God knows you don't deserve more. But you persist, so I'm going to tell you. Madli wasn't corrupted by me. Nor by Saigon. She was corrupted by love, her love for another man."

"Rubbish! She couldn't... She wouldn't..."

"Hark at him!" Betty cried. "Whatever makes him think that Madli couldn't, wouldn't or shouldn't love another man?"

"His bloated ego, that's what," Jill drawled. "Men are full of it."

"It's the truth, Paul," Wilma said quietly.

"If you're so damn sure," he challenged suspiciously, "who the hell was he?"

"A rogue," she answered, swirling the ice in her glass and smiling slightly. "A handsome, worldly, ruthless rogue. Extremely likeable. A man's man and a woman's man. A new conquest was like slipping on a fresh shirt. He was after Madli the moment he set eyes on her. When he did succeed it happened rather abruptly, I thought, as though it was her doing... He let it go on for nearly three months. Unusually long for his affairs. She seemed quite devastated when he ended it, so I felt. For quite a while she withdrew into herself, moody and remote. Then suddenly she emerged as charming and carefree as ever. Yet far more adventurous, and daring. It was the beginning of the woman we buried a few hours ago."

"Wilma..."

"I'm sorry, Paul. I often wondered how you couldn't have known. Of course you were away a lot, and I guess our friends in Saigon were kinder than I gave them credit."

"...who the hell was he?"

"Does it matter? It was long ago. And dear Madli is gone, may she rest in peace."

"He should be here with the rest of us," Freddy said morosely.

She smiled and finished her drink. "He'd like that, I think. I know I'd like another drink. Jim? Would you mind, dear? Gin and a bit of tonic, please... Perhaps we should all join the bottle brigade of Paul, Freddy and Carl. Saves a lot of trips to the bar. Which reminds me, Carl. Remember the night you met Madli and me in the bar of the Caravelle Hotel in Saigon? Seems ages..."

He chuckled. "All my table bombed out of our minds and in you walk."

"It was Uncle Dick," Meg said flatly.

Betty turned quickly to Wilma. "Your husband and Madli...?"

She bit her lip. "Meg, there was no need, my dear."

"Dick...?" Paul whispered hoarsely, looking stunned when Meg touched his hand and nodded. "I can't believe it. Such a nice fellow..."

"Aren't we all?" Ward murmured.

"When did you know, Wilma?" Maria asked.

"At the start. I usually do."

"Why did you put up with it?"

"I love him. I've loved him since I was a child. We married at eighteen. Our la-di-da families disapproved and cut us off, so we went it alone, scraping by on my typist's pay while he struggled through law school. But there was fun and laughter..."

She accepted her drink from Jim and raised it. "And when he was on his way and times were good, we drank life to the full and savoured every drop." She took a sip and rested the glass on an arm of her chair. "He was unfaithful early on, and often ever since. Horribly shattering at first. I wanted to die. But slowly I submitted. It couldn't be helped. I am consoled by the knowledge that he loves me, and would never forsake me for another woman."

"But you could leave him, surely?" Maria pressed fretfully.

"To what end? He needs me, and I need him. His little affairs rarely last very long. Afterwards, we get along famously. We like books, music, theatre, travel, people. We like one another. We share many memories. I wouldn't trade them for anything in the world. Nor him..." She touched the loose skin under her chin. "And one day I shall have him all to myself."

"But all those other women!" Maria persisted. "How do you feel towards them?"

"Murderous. He's my man, dammit."

"Madli too?"

"I did for a while... I don't think she was aware that I knew of their affair, though now and then I felt her looking at me as if appealing for understanding. Strange, isn't it?"

"Every word of it," Maria sighed. "I don't understand. I know I couldn't bear the hurt if a husband of mine betrayed me." And with a troubled glance at Jim: "I would never be able to forgive, I'm sure."

"Never say never, my dear girl," Wilma told her gently. "You might find yourself a prisoner of love, a willing prisoner. Then you'd forgive. I did... And Dick is quite thoughtful in his way. He felt it would be awkward for me if he came to Bangkok while Madli was here. That's why we had that tryst in Hong Kong every month or so. Now that Madli is gone, I dare say you will meet him at last."

Getting up from her chair a little unsteadily, she set her glass on the table, smoothed the wrinkled skirt over her full hips, and glanced around wearily. "I feel a bit groggy, so if you don't mind I shall freshen up. A cold shower is usually good for a new lease of life. Now drink up, and help yourselves to Alun's leftovers in the fridge if you feel peckish."

And pausing at her bedroom door, her hand on the knob and her open gaze on Somsak, she said, "I was asleep here when dear Madli died. You must take my word for it, Somsak. I have no one to vouch for me. My husband is the only man I have ever taken to my bed." She entered the room and silently closed the door behind her.

"I never suspected," Paul muttered.

"Our little Miss Know-it-all did," said Jill, glaring at Meg.

"Poor Wilma," Beatrice sighed. "Such a cross to bear."

"She's marvellous," said Susan.

"She's too forgiving," Maria humphed.

"She's in love," said Ward. "It's good to know it can last."

Betty caught Paul's hazy eye.

"Satisfied?" she taunted.

Chapter Ten

"Some lady, ain't she?" Carl gloated, grinning as he settled back against the buffet, elbows braced on top, a bottle of Scotch in hand. "Fuckin' good looker too. A cryin' shame it has to go to waste while that asshole screws his way round 'Nam. And like she says, it's Saigon where I met Madli, not here as you might've figured. I stay at the Caravelle on our triangle run, Bangkok to Vientiane to Saigon and back to Bangkok. Me and my crew were tryin' to drink the bar dry when in she walks with Wilma. The joint was jammed -"

"With drunken newsmen as usual," Betty gibed.

"We're by the door. They join our table. I can't believe my luck. A classy blonde with a great body's comin' on to me. I didn't lose any time, I tell ya'..." And squinting at Noi and Dang, asleep in the arms of Jill and Frank: "Thai, Laotians, Vietnamese. For years that's all I got into. Prettiest little dolls in the world but I nearly wore it out lookin' for one really good in the sack. Know what I mean, Jim...?"

"Oh, I don't know."

"Oh yes you do," Maria sniffed. "You know a couple of dozen at least. Nit says -"

"So! What are you paying that God damn Nit?"

"Blame yourself! You keep her in juicy gossip by bringing your little tramps to that house!"

"It's my house, for Christ's sake!"

"Shame on you, Jim," Ward tushed. "You're robbing our short-time hotels of a rich trade."

"I say there ain't a real good screw in a carload," Carl grumbled.

"Stop it!" Maria cried.

"Stop screwin'?"

"Stop talking like that!"

"Grin and bear it, Maria," said Betty wearily. "Carl's choice of language sums up his noble life."

"Disgusting!"

"The children..." Beatrice began, taking her eyes off her wheezing husband to glance tenderly at Tim, asleep with his head on his school bag, and Meg, an arm on her father's knee and her empty gaze on her mother's friends.

"They heard it all before," said Jill lightly. "Right, Paul?"

He sipped his whisky, glaring at her over the glass.

"Had you known Wilma before, Carl?" Susan wondered.

"First time I saw either of 'em. Madli asked could they sit with us. I was greased lightnin' gettin' a chair under that great ass. We got together on most trips. Hell, she wanted same as me. We did it damn well. But it wasn't just..." He looked again at Noi and Dang, shaking his head. "They got nothin' to say. Not a fuckin' thing. You heard Noi with the spook a while ago... (and mimicking her squeak), 'You like Thailand? You like Thai food? You like Thai guhl?'..."

Jim laughed and he grinned. "Yeah, and the Vietnamese the same, though there's more harpin' on money. Right off they ask 'how much you make?', then tell ya' a lota' ways to make a pile, all God damn crooked of course. 'You make too much money marry me we go Ameleecah'." He snorted and took a swig from the bottle. "But they look after ya', these little girls. Fuckin' right they do. Some of their *farang* guys can never again take up with a round eye. They got somethin'..." He exchanged a knowing grin with Frank. "That hair, long, black, shiny. Bright eyes, trustin' and lovin'. Laughter like a schoolgirl's. Graceful as Queen Sirikit herself. And their skin. Soft brown like the spook's though I never felt like screwin' her..."

"You wouldn't get to first base," she cracked.

"...and their touch. Christ. Little hands flutterin' away like butterflies. And most of 'em look like kids."

"There's a Humbert Humbert in every last one of you," Betty jeered.

"And all of us on the prowl for a precious Lolita," Ward leered comically.

"Six years ago they saved my sanity," Carl growled, jabbing with the bottle. "I just wound up a hitch with a Denver bitch. Phoney Mormon do-gooder. Acted like her crap didn't stink. In bed it was like rammin' a knot hole. My fifth marriage down the drain. I couldn't look at another white broad. And I couldn't get enough of these little dolls. I soaked it up..."

Another belt from the bottle and he smiled to himself, eyes half closed. "All that jazz under their big mosquito nets... A little girl in Udorn, no more'n seventeen, used to sit on my chest bare assed and fan me and feed me mango and sticky rice. Lovin' and happy-go-lucky but touchy as hell. One rough word and she'd bawl her head off. 'You no love me no moah'..." He chuckled. "I liked watchin' 'em get ready for work. Squeezin' into tight mini skirts, and high heels that just about crippled 'em. Pilin' up their hair and stuffin' their tiny tits into padded bras. A little beauty in Tahklee used to say 'solly, Cahl, *mai mee nome*, no have tit'. Before headin' out she'd *wai* to a Buddha in a glass case plastered with gold leaf and surrounded by flowers and joss sticks and tell me 'Buddha say I make too much money tonight'."

"You're talking about cheap bar girls," Betty scoffed.

"They're the best kind. But they got nothin' to say. A bit of kiddin' back and forth. That's it. I was walkin' round with pretty little dummies and it got so I didn't know what to do with 'em. Sometimes I ached for a good shoutin' match with that Denver bitch." He paused, thinking. "What a difference that Madli. She was some woman. Interested in who I was, what I did, what I felt. She had me talkin' my head off. Even in bed. And in bed it was like I'd never known a good piece -"

"Did you know about Paul?" Betty cut in.

He shrugged. "A lota' *farang* wives go hungry here. They start lookin' for it. You don't ask why. You don't ask nobody's business in these parts if you're smart." He glanced at Paul. "Yeah, I knew about him. I found out about the kids when I caught up with her in Bangkok. Come to think of it, I didn't know a whole lot about Madli. I learned more tonight than I did before. She was more for tellin' about the crazy times she had with you guys. I can still hear that accent. I could listen for hours."

"Do you have children, Carl?" Susan wondered.

"Four. They're with their mothers, I guess."

"I have a daughter," said Freddy earnestly. "A fine little girl she is too. She's nine now. Name's Wendy. Lives in Melbourne with her mother, who was once my wife."

"Poor kid doesn't know what she's missing," Jill mocked.

"Hey, what's this?" Carl muttered, contemplating Freddy. "I think his fuckin' bottle's empty."

Freddy held it to the light and gasped. "By God! So it is. Do you think...?"

Carl pulled a bottle of gin from a case and dropped it in his lap.

"Forgive him, dear Lord," Betty prayed. "He knows not what devilish mischief he's done."

"A little ice, if you will," said Freddy grandly, handing Carl his glass and empty bottle.

Standing the empty on the table, he scooped ice cubes into the glass from the bucket and delivered it with a clumsy bow.

"I like children, don't you, Carl?" Freddy confided, the glass clutched in the crook of his elbow as he wrestled with the bottle cap.

"Never had time for 'em. I'm a bush pilot, for fuck's sake. Couldn't make it with the airlines. Pilots with big thirsts scare the shit out of 'em." He grinned and took a belt from his bottle. "Anyhow, I had a bellyful of rules in the airforce in Korea. Bush flyin' pays good, but you're all over hell's half acre and livin' in God-forsaken holes. Not many women can take it. Sure, they're game till you're hooked. Then they want to squat on their ass in some lousy suburb and stuff themselves fat. I took a 'breed girl off her daddy's trap lines in Alaska. After their crummy cabin my shack in the city looked pretty good. She settles in, and when I wanta' move on fuckin' dynamite couldn't budge her."

Jill snorted. "I suppose you ditched her like you abandoned your stupid wives and bloody brats."

He laughed. "Serves 'em fuckin' right. I was lookin' for a woman who'd follow a man clear to the gates of hell. I thought I'd found her in Madli."

"She was trying to make it on her own," said Betty.

"And she did," said Maria promptly.

"She was reckless. Soon as we picked up where we'd left off in Saigon she had me smuggle her on some flights to Vientiane. That's where Jim met her."

"But I thought -" Maria began before Jim interrupted: "In the American commissary. I'd just got their liquor account. Hadn't seen you in weeks."

Carl chuckled. "Wasn't me brought ya' runnin' with your tongue hangin' out. Anyway, we got the same deal in Vientiane, Saigon and

Bangkok. Park at the end of the runway. No customs crap. No questions asked. She could buy what she liked."

"Like opium and gold bars?" Jill suggested slyly.

"Like Beatrice said. French perfume, cigarettes, wine, liqueurs, underwear. You see the price on that junk in Bangkok? Next thing I know she's flyin' with me on supply drops to the hill tribes on our side in Laos and 'Nam. Had to cut that out, though. Too fuckin' risky after one of our planes was shot down and the crew killed or captured. God knows how Uncle Ho's Migs got onto 'em. They were Johnny-on-the-spot. You might've met the guys at one of Madli's parties. She bawled her eyes out when they cashed in their chips."

"Did the CIA mind you taking your girlfriend on those flights?" Betty asked casually.

"Why the hell should they?"

"They're your boss, aren't they?"

He shrugged. "I'm paid by Unistates Air. It was their fuckin' newspaper ad back home that got me into this. They wanted old airforce pilots to fly cargo in the Far East. That's all. I know nothin' about the CIA."

"Who do you think is arming the anti-commie hill tribes in Laos and Vietnam?"

"The Salvation Army maybe?"

"Very funny. I still say Unistates Air is CIA."

"You'd never prove it," he said, grinning craftily. "We're phantoms. Our planes ain't marked. Our pilots ain't registered. Our orders from Unistates Air ain't on paper. But I'll tell ya' this much. Anti-commie guerrillas are everywhere the US ain't supposed to go, and it helps Uncle Sam in 'Nam if they get guns, ammo, explosives, radios and maps, and somebody to show 'em how to use it. The US Air Force can't be caught at it, so somebody sets up a phoney cargo airline and hires a bunch of loony pilots willin' to take big risks for big bucks. But nobody wants to -"

"Should you be telling us this if it's supposed to be secret?" Susan asked uneasily.

"Secret?" he grunted. "Shit. What I tell ya' don't matter a fuck 'cause we don't exist. Like I was sayin', nobody wants to know us. Ask the US embassy who we are and what we do. Ask the Thai government. They play dumb. They have to. They can't interfere.

And the cops can't touch us for any shit we raise. That burns your ass, eh, Somsak...?" His insolent smirk missed the mark as Somsak concentrated on the drink he was pouring. "And them's orders. From the CIA? I don't know and I don't wanta' know. All I care is I make a fistful of dough and can get away with murder."

"You haven't got away with this murder," Jill said pointedly.

He sucked in a deep breath and expelled it. "Hell, I wanted Madli to ditch everythin' and come to Costa Rica. Warm climate. Soft life. Good flyin' jobs. Big bucks if you run drugs, or guns to the revolutions in the neighbourhood. But I'd have cooled it if I'd had her. Not a chance. She was livin' it up here like it all would end tomorrow. There were too many of us. And Madli didn't belong to one man."

"She belonged to me for many years," Paul murmured, red-eyed over his glass.

"No wonder she flipped," said Jill.

"She knew what she was doin'," said Carl. "She called the shots. Soon as I got too eager she put me on hold like some others. I got a key. Didn't get to use it enough to suit me, so she set me up with starvin' *farang* wives. After her they were dead fish."

"Sure one of those *farang* wives wasn't my Paddi?" Ward asked lightly.

"Couldn't tell, Ward," Carl replied deadpan. "A lota' *farang* wives look alike to me."

"Just wondering if you deserve my sympathy. I guess you do, Carl."

"He deserves the rope if he did in Madli," said Betty, squinting up at Carl. "I can see the headline: 'Repulsed suitor slays playgirl'. And what a story of sex and intrigue in the fleshpots of Southeast Asia! Tell us why you did it, killer Carl."

"No man in his right mind would rub out the best piece of ass he ever knew, for fuck's sake!"

"You bloody scoundrel!" Paul exploded, his face flushed with anger. "Tell Somsak where you were at the time my wife was murdered!"

"None of his fuckin' business."

"Tell *us* then," Betty whispered loudly behind her hand. "Quickly. While Somsak studies the ceiling."

"Ain't much to tell. I picked up a skinful of booze in the Patpong bars till maybe two in the mornin'. They never forget me. That buck-tooth bitch I brought from Lopburi to do my laundry can fill in the rest. She's fuckin' useless in bed but she sure can massage. Around two-thirty or so she's runnin' up and down my back in her bare feet."

Jim roared and he watched, chuckling.

"Stop encouraging him!" Maria stormed. "His servant will tell the police anything he wants her to!"

"What the hell do you mean?" Jim demanded, suddenly grim. "Are you accusing Carl of killing Madli? Are you accusing him of lying?"

"I caught you in a lie. You told me you met Madli at the Royal Bangkok Sports Club. Now you say you met her in the American commissary in Vientiane. I want you to tell all of us, here and now, about your affair with that woman!"

"Oh, no." He got up from the sofa, slowly shaking his head. "No you don't." He drained his glass and put it on the table. "You're crazy if you think I'd give you a chance to tear into every God damn thing I had to say." He looked down at Susan. "Wilma said there was grub...?"

"Yes. Alun's leftovers in the fridge."

"I'm hungry. I'll eat out there." He stepped over Ward's legs and picked up the ice bucket on his way to the courtyard doorway. "I guess we can use more ice."

He was in the courtyard when Maria hissed, "Coward!"

His shout came back: "JEALOUS BITCH!"

Chapter Eleven

Nervously sipping her watery Scotch, Maria glanced around regretfully. "I'm sorry. I shouldn't go on like this at Jim. Yet I do it more and more now, and I can't seem to stop."

"It is a bit much," said Betty. "What's the use? He is what he is. You can't remake him."

"But he should be honest with me. And with himself. He doesn't understand. The life he leads could ruin his reputation. Face is very important when you're in business here. His companies might let him go if they heard about all those women he -"

"Nonsense," said Jill. "Jim sells the products of breweries and distilleries on the other side of the world. They don't give a hoot how many women he sleeps with here. It's the barrels of booze that count."

"He damages his health, though," she insisted, placing her glass on the table and clasping her hands. "You must have noticed that twitch in his left eye. And he complains about a pain. Here, by the kidneys. I read that too much sex can damage your sight and kidneys. My seer says it's happening to Jim."

"Your *what*?!" Betty laughed.

"Her seer," said Ward. "Consulting a seer is quite an ancient Thai custom. The prime minister even puts off important decisions till his seer, the Buddhist patriarch, tells him when the moment is favourable. And many *farangs* whose families have been here for ages rely on seers as well."

"Maybe Somsak's seer can tell him who killed Madli," Betty suggested artfully.

"I don't think so, Miss Betty," he replied, smiling broadly.

"Then let's try Maria's seer. He sounds like an expert on sex."

"He's very wise," Maria said reverently. "It's the spirit of King Chulalongkorn. He speaks through a very respected medium, an old lady in Thonburi."

"And he was a very respected king," said Susan. "I was in high school when I read that book about Anna Leonowens, the English woman who taught the children of old King Monkut. Chulalongkorn was the little crown prince. He became a most enlightened monarch. The Thai say he brought their backward country into the twentieth century."

"He certainly was an expert on sex," said Betty. "The young devil had ninety-eight wives, so they say."

"And what else besides sex do Maria and the King of Siam talk about?" Jill wanted to know.

"He gives me advice, mostly. He told me when it was the right time to move out of my parents' home into an apartment of my own, and when to buy my car and take my holidays. He knows if the omens are good or bad. He also warns me of the people I shouldn't trust."

"How the hell did he miss Jim?"

"He wants to see Jim. He says he can help him. But Jim won't go. He says it's bad enough having me lecture him about his morals without having my seer on his back." She sighed deeply. "He lies so much. He told me it was all over with him and Madli long ago. But only last month he took her on a sales trip to American bases up-country. Nit told me, and I told my seer. He said Madli was bad for Jim."

"I beg to differ," said Ward. "And with all due respect for old Chulalongkorn. Madli was good for Jim. She was the first worldly woman in his life. He craved her sophistication, probably hoping it would rub off on him. And he was in seventh heaven when she let him share her limelight at times. She also helped open a few doors that were good for his business. Embassy commissaries and private club bars, for instance."

"Give Jim his due as well," Susan said earnestly. "He made it on his own in Bangkok. It took hard work and determination."

"You're damn right," said Carl. "When I met him a few years ago he didn't have a pot to piss in. He told me he hitch-hiked round the world and was down to his last coupla' bucks when he blew into town."

"It's true. For weeks he slept in the free cells at Buddhist temples and I suspect he went hungry a lot. He got his break when that American rental agency on Ploenchit Road took him on. He made money for them, and their recommendation got him the companies he sells for now. Jim's quite well off today."

"Not so remarkable," Betty said dryly. "Bangkok has endless opportunities for *farangs* with any get-up-and-go. Jim got here when those little wars in the neighbourhood opened things up. In on the ground floor, as it were. Not bad, I suppose, for a rather gauche young man from the American mid-west."

"He still is," Jill sneered. "He believes all that crap about Bangkok's so-called jet set. He thinks it's people like us, so he must be seen with us in certain cocktail bars and restaurants, at tiresome embassy affairs, at places like Wilma's for the weekend booze-up, and by the pool at the Royal Bangkok Sports Club with the other hangovers on Sunday. That's where he meets those idle bloody daughters of the veddy veddy rich Thai. Getting them to bed makes him feel he's arrived in the arms of the upper class."

"There are so many of them," Maria sighed. "Nit says they constantly phone and send little gifts. I suppose each believes she's the only one. Nit says he once arranged to have four girls come to the house at different times on the same day. He took them all to bed."

Carl whistled softly. "Now that's damn fine humpin'."

"He drops them suddenly, cruelly. It must hurt. Nit says there's always some young woman on the phone in tears."

"Stupid little bitches," Jill murmured, looking tenderly on Noi's sweet repose. "But let them learn. They've got to learn."

"Yet he wouldn't stop seeing Madli when I begged him to. Why did he have to go on and on with her?"

"She was his ticket to the dress circle," Betty said simply. "So he hung on even after his demotion to her platoon of surplus men. And he didn't fare badly. Jim was one of a very few to get a key to the goodies, and now and then he had her to himself on trips to American bases. Still, for someone who likes to lord it over women, it must have been galling to become just another of Madli's obedient little puppets."

"She made her own, you know," said Freddy, intently pouring gin into his glass, then settling back to a long, slow drink.

"Made her own what, for God's sake?" Jill demanded impatiently.

He looked up, surprised. "Her own little puppets, of course. Delightful little puppets. I was at tiny Tim's birthday party a while ago. Many children came, Thai and *farang*. Some were Tim's classmates at Ruam Rudee. And Madli put on a puppet show on the lawn. She made the sets and all the little people and their costumes. She worked the strings and spoke all the parts. Of course everyone had an Estonian accent. I can still hear the little hero's piping voice: 'Rumpled sheepskin, throw down a chair!'..."

Susan laughed. "I think you mean 'Rapunzel, let down your hair'."

"Enchanting..." And squinting in Paul's direction: "I say, old man. I put together that little electric train you sent Tim for his birthday. But the transformer didn't work."

"Transformer?" Paul mumbled tiredly.

"Not to worry, dear fellow. I had Seato's engineering school fix it. Works fine now. Madli and Tim and I had hours of fun with that little train." He settled back, absorbed by his drink once more.

Maria smiled faintly. "I didn't know that side of her. Yet I must say she was quite friendly when Jim took me to her parties. She seemed grateful to me for some reason. I never understood why. But she had an aura, a presence. It made me feel inadequate. I couldn't like her. I didn't want to like her. I wish Jim hadn't loved her so."

"Jim love a woman?" Betty scoffed. "He doesn't know how. With him it's a matter of pursuit, persuasion and conquest. And surely he never dreamed he'd find so much easy prey in one place, Thai and *farang*."

"His latest *farang* is an American army wife," Maria said unhappily. "Her name's Sharon. Her husband is a colonel and an adviser to the Thai army. One day her chauffeur came for Jim and he told Nit who she was and where she lived. I went to see her. She was very nice. We had tea on her terrace. I told her about Jim and me and asked her to please leave him alone. She was upset. She hadn't known about me. She asked me to be patient. She'd soon be going home. She said her husband was obsessed with Thai girls and hadn't touched her in two years. She said she took Jim out of need."

"There are such things," Betty whispered.

"Did you confront Madli as well?" Susan asked.

Maria shook her head. "She frightened me."

"Was Maria deluded?" Jill mused. "Was Madli her scapegoat for all the Sharons and little Thai dolls? Did she think they'd vanish, and she'd have Jim to herself, if she could break Madli's hold on him at last?"

"Give up this man," Susan urged. "It's destroying you."

The deep brown eyes clouded and a hand strayed nervously to the raven hair. "I love him," she said timidly. "He's the first and only one with me. We met at Pattaya. He came to my table when I was dining at Barbo's. We talked and laughed for hours, and all next day we swam and water-skied together. I was ever so happy when he invited me to dinner at his home in Bangkok. I never meant to go so far. But I felt this wonderful love for him, and I thought he loved me, and it just seemed to happen..."

"It's not the end of the world," said Susan gently. "Put it behind you, Maria. You must."

She rubbed her thighs and shook her head distressfully. "You don't understand. We are Greeks. And Greeks are Greeks wherever they live. They have a strict moral code and family tradition. My parents are very strict. I was sent to St. Joseph's Convent School. It was quite a concession when they let me have my own apartment while I'm single. A husband is another matter...."

"Would they let you marry Jim?"

"They don't know about Jim. They want me to marry a Greek, and they favour a young man in Corinth, our family's ancestral home. He stayed with us in Bangkok once. I haven't agreed to marry him. It's out of the question now anyway. No nice Greek boy would marry a Greek girl who can't hang out the bedsheet on the morning after the wedding."

"The *bedsheet*?" Jill repeated amusingly.

"It's very Greek," Betty explained. "Nice girls must be able to show they were virgins when they married by hanging out the bedsheet with the evidence."

"What a stupid bloody custom."

Ward grinned. "I dare say the nosy relatives and neighbours can be fooled by a little chicken blood on the sheet."

"Bridegrooms too, do you think?" Betty wondered innocently.

"Some, perhaps," he replied airily. "Certainly not the suspicious types like myself."

"Clever devil," she said, tossing a bottle cap into his lap.

"I was never a liar or dishonest," Maria said, her lips quivering. "Now I lie to my parents about where I go and what I do so they won't find out about Jim. I would do anything for him so I've been dishonest too. My family handles a lot of shipping in and out of

Bangkok. I work in our office. I look after the manifests on the cargo that's on its way here. They're confidential, but I've been making copies for Jim. He asked for them. He wouldn't say why, and I didn't press him. I was afraid for him."

"The little crook!" Jill exclaimed. "I think I know what he's up to. You can buy anything on the thieves' market here, sometimes while it's still at sea. A manifest tells what's arriving on what ship. The thieves sneak aboard and lower the stuff into their speedboats before the watchman's counted his bribe. No wonder Jim's driving a Mercedes."

"I suspect there might be an entirely different explanation," Ward said thoughtfully.

"Yes," said Susan. "Let's not make hasty judgements. But Maria, be honest with yourself. Don't count on Jim. He won't change. You're a lovely young woman, and you deserve much better."

"And Jim? How do I get over Jim? He has all my love, though he ridicules it and tries to destroy it. He talks horribly about us. He makes me do horrid things. Last week he brought a Thai girl to my apartment and made me go to bed with them..."

She trembled, suddenly aware that he stood in the courtyard doorway, swinging the ice bucket by the handle and chewing a toothpick; he glared relentlessly at her.

"What other fucking crap has she been telling you?!" he demanded savagely.

"The works!" Jill snarled. "How you killed Madli to shut her up when she caught you trying to get into her God damn daughter and I don't put it past you, you bastard."

He spat out the toothpick. "Maria might have killed her, the jealous bitch. Tonight wasn't the first time she wished her dead. But I'm her alibi..."

Maria tensed. "Jim. Please. She's joking."

"Your alibi," he slowly repeated, his lip curling. "I can't get rid of you, can I? You sat on it all those years as if you didn't know what it's for and just because I showed you..."

"Don't talk about us, Jim! Please, Jim! Please don't...!"

"...you think you own me." He glanced round the circle. "We spent all that night in bed. I left it in for hours."

She clapped her hands over her ears. "No! No! Please..."

"Yes! Yes!" Carl roared, struggling erect from his slouch against the buffet. "Jim was humpin' this goody-goody from some asshole convent while our poor Madli was drawin' her last fuckin' breath! Ain't that what you said, Jim?"

"She's too self righteous to admit it. I'm just her jocker, for Christ's sake. The only way I can stop her whining about my 'immoral life', as she calls it, is to ram it into her."

"No, Jim. Please..." Her pale face contorted and her cry fell to a whimper. "Please don't, Jim..."

Susan pulled the sobbing, shaking body into her arms.

"My God. What are you doing to one another?" Wilma stood bewildered at her bedroom door in a long, loose robe of blue Thai silk, her face puffy and without make-up, her bobbed black hair damp and clinging from the shower. She moved slowly into the room, shaking her head despairingly at the sight of Maria's agony.

"Why must you hurt each other?" She stopped by Carl, her clear blue eyes questioning; he splashed Scotch into his glass and stared at it. She gazed sorrowfully at Jim; head down, he dropped the ice bucket by the table and sat heavily in the bamboo chair next to Jill.

She sighed. "I've never seen you like this before. It's frightening." Sinking slowly into her arm chair, she looked anxiously from one to the other of her friends.

Freddy met her gaze, smiling sadly. Somsak watched Ward blow softly on the ash of his cigar till it glowed. Beatrice pressed a hand to her mouth, her eyes fearful. Frank kept his eyes on the girl in his arms and Jill soothed Noi's sleepy murmurs. Betty reached for Wilma's hand and held it tightly.

"Well, Paul," said Wilma. "What else have you achieved?"

He looked at her vacantly and didn't reply.

All that could be heard now were Maria's muffled sobs and the wheezing whistle of the slumbering Reverend Ralph.

PART TWO

Chapter Twelve

Somsak felt the weight of the hours. His eyelids were heavy and his mouth tacky, and he had a crick in his neck from sitting in the same position on the sofa for too long. He envied Noi and Dang; they were deep in a sleep that had been only slightly disturbed by high voices now and then. It would be easy to drift off as they had done, and he wondered if he had dozed for a few seconds without realising it, which sometimes happened at *farang* parties if they became too much for him. He marvelled at the *farang's* capacity for drink and late hours; here it was nearly three in the morning and only the Reverend Ralph was out of it.

He lit a cigarette and savoured the smoke. For a while there had been some moving about to stretch legs and use the bathrooms; and some muted, desultory talk that slowly petered out. Now a silence had descended, an oddly comforting and welcome silence. It reminded him of an observation that Madli had made about gatherings that go on till very late. She had said it was quite uncanny, but at a certain hour there came a reprieve from talk and laughter; a moment when everyone withdrew into themselves and their thoughts and seemed oblivious to those around them. This was such a moment, he felt. He looked about him...

Freddy hummed softly to himself, keeping time with his bottle and glass on the padded arms of his easy chair. Wilma seemed charmed by the cigarette smoke curling from Jill's wide nostrils, and Betty, still on the other cushion at Wilma's feet, combed her rich auburn hair over the left breast of her yellow cotton frock and dropped strands from the comb into an ashtray. On the bamboo chair on Jill's right, Jim thumbed through a National Geographic he had found on one of the lamp tables outside the circle. Next to him, Carl sprawled over the buffet, eating with a spoon from a large bowl of pilaff he had foraged from the kitchen and washing down the spicy rice and meat with Scotch. Ward watched him through whiffs of cigar smoke from his place on the floor in front of the wide sofa; and beside Somsak on the sofa, Maria clung to Susan's hand, her breath tremulous and her eyes red from weeping.

Somsak's gaze wandered up the room. On the stair landing, Frank leaned against the wall with his legs stretched out and played with the long braid of the sleeping girl in his arms. Beatrice was back on her bamboo chair by the landing after wiping her husband's drooling lips and settling little Tim on a pillow where he slept, hugging his school bag, by his father's easy chair. Paul slumped in the chair, his face grey and creased and his tired eyes on Meg; she had an arm on his knee, her slender legs drawn up under her school skirt on the cushion, and her vacant gaze on her mother's friends and lovers.

Somsak wondered why Paul had allowed himself and Meg to suffer the taunts against him, and the painful descriptions of the woman they loved. Had he been prepared to put up with that in this curious attempt to find her killer? He stubbed out his cigarette. He wished it had been left to him. He believed... There was sudden movement.

Ward had got quickly to his feet and dropped the remains of his cigar in an ashtray. Under bland stares he hitched up his trousers, scowled comically, and trotted up and down the room a few times on the balls of his stockinged feet; then he uncapped a bottle of Scotch and one of gin and topped every glass around the circle with extravagant flourish. He carried his own glass to the wall of screen windows and peered out on the darkened garden; taking a short drink, he closed his eyes and breathed deeply.

"Ah, yes," he sighed contentedly. "The best time of the day. It's not too hot. I'm barely perspiring, no thanks to our wobbly old fan up there. I see it's expired again. No matter. A lovely breeze brings us the jasmine's perfume from Wilma's garden. Breezes are rare in Bangkok, as you're well aware. Apparently this one is caused by that tall block of flats next door. An architect at one of our parties here told me it creates a slight wind current over Wilma's compound. I don't understand the principle but thank heaven for small mercies.

"Now listen to the bullfrogs in Wilma's *klong*. Noisy little blighters, aren't they? It's their loudest hour, and perhaps their finest too. All that croaking is supposed to have something to do with procreation."

Scratching the screen with a thumbnail, he whistled softly, "Thank God for this. There must be dozens of mosquitoes on the mesh. Blood-thirsty devils. What a feast they'd have in here, though I'm sure they'd get blotto on our veins. Most Thai don't have screens on their windows, you know. They burn Chinese mosquito coils after sundown and escape under mosquito nets at bedtime. Their wooden shutters are closed against the sun's hottest rays in the day, and again overnight to keep out the *kamoy*. They bathe in rain water from huge *klong* jars, lounge about in sarong or *phakoma*, and cook outdoors with utensils of stone and cast iron. Simple lives in simple homes. The only drawback is their toilet, that ceramic hole in the floor one must squat over. Very Asian and quite dreadful. Yet I like old Thai houses. They have a marvellous aroma of spices and polished wood. I've always wanted to live in one..."

He drank slowly and thoughtfully. "I loathe our ugly apartment in Ambassador Court, cluttered as it is with heavy and overstuffed furniture that Paddi insisted on shipping from England at great public expense. Of course every room has an air conditioner. She won't try to put up with the heat. Just as well, perhaps. An hour in the midday sun and she comes unstuck. Hair, clothes, make-up. Like a blob of steaming white putty." He grimaced. "Hideous...

"She seldom goes out if she can't have my official air-conditioned car and chauffeur. It takes her to expensive air-conditioned shops in Gaysorn to squander my wages on everything of poor taste, to air-conditioned beauty salons for layers of costly camouflage, and to pretentious air-conditioned restaurants for luncheons of dull Western dishes at exorbitant prices."

He faced the room, shaking his head. "Do you know, I don't believe Paddi has tasted Thai food. Not surprising, really. We've been here four years and she has yet to wander the noisy, colourful markets, the peaceful temples, the lush gardens and haunting ruins. She turns up her nose at the beauty of the *Loi Krathong* festival of lights, Thai classic dancing and music, and the candlelight processions of *Visakha Puja* for the Lord Buddha. She doesn't want to know the fun of the *Songkran* water festival and kite flying by the Grand Palace in the strong winds of February, or the joy of the lively celebrations on the king's birthday. She misses so much. Many other *farangs* do as well. Such a pity..."

He listened for a moment. "Hear that? The bullfrog symphony has been joined by the crickets. Together they make enough noise to waken the dead. And our dead is so briefly buried. Buried in Bangkok. How long before a corpse rots in the ground here, do you think? Horrible thought. We must get Madli out of the ground and have her cremated. We might scatter her ashes over her beloved cliffs and meadows of home. Which reminds me..."

He grinned mischievously. "When I was in officer's school at Sandhurst, a classmate gassed himself over a disastrous love affair, and a few of us followed the wish in his farewell note and took his ashes up in a small cabin plane to sprinkle over his beloved Berkshire. We got thoroughly stinko, and without thinking we opened the box of ash by an open window rather than over the side. The whole lot blew back in our faces, and for hours we were spitting out powdered bits of our dear departed chum. Right. My last cremation story for tonight. I promise..."

He glanced round the circle, thoughtful now. "Buried in Bangkok... I suppose we all are in one way or another. But buried mostly in a life of indulgence we could never dream of finding in our narrow, boring plots at home. And what has it done to us? I'm thinking of Jim's sterling performance a while ago. Once I might have objected. I didn't. But why? Because we expect little better of one another? We and our many absent playmates are together a lot. We serve insults and taunts with idle gossip, one-liners, laughter and drinks. Anything goes. Suddenly one of our more delicate companions is terribly hurt by thoughtless outbursts. Yet we mustn't blame anybody. This is what has become of us. Accept it, and don't sell Maria short. She'll recover. We're like reeds. Bent by misfortune's winds we spring up again as strong as ever. And so, Maria..."

Stepping to the side of the sofa, he raised his glass. "Drink up, dear girl. Let the warm booze melt the chill that seized your heart. Be strong. Somewhere a loving and faithful man waits to make you his wife."

She smiled shyly, hesitated, then reached for her Scotch and took a tentative sip. He nodded encouragingly, and scanned the silent but attentive circle, his grey eyes alight when they dwelt on Betty. She passed the comb through the auburn hair once more and stuck out the tip of her tongue. He grinned.

"My, you do look lovely, Betty," he said approvingly. "Warm and glowing, as women should be in the morning. Contented and secretive too, as though fresh from a lover's arms. I'm glad you wear your hair long, and I dare say you like it to be touched. Many women do, I know. Madli did. She almost purred with pleasure when I stroked that soft yellow cloud. It went so well with the golden brown of her lovely body. She worshipped the sun as Baltic people will. Much of their year is frozen over. She sunbathed at every chance, and quite often at Bangsaen, one of the wealthy Thais' beach retreats on the gulf. Few *farangs* go there. Madli braved the hot sand in her bikini while pampered Thai women lounged in the shade of those huge trees on the promenade. They believe, as Chinese women do, that beauty is a light skin..."

Smiling to himself, he returned to the screen window. "The tiny fair hairs on Madli's arms shone in the sun. She would blow them, and laugh at her childish whim. I seemed to hear quite a lot about her childhood. It must have been very happy. Her grandfather and mother were loving but rather strait-laced. Much of Madli's life spun around her father, an aesthetic, humorous and learned man of books, stories, dreams and fantasies. A fine teacher but quite hopeless around their farm. He'd run off with Madli to the meadows, woods, and the cliffs by the sea. There they created a fairyland of joy and devotion that would haunt her forever..."

He gazed sympathetically at Meg, her eyes on him now as he recalled her mother. "Meg knows. For I'm sure her love for her mother is as deep and lasting as Madli's love for her father." He looked away. "What became of him, I wonder? Many people vanished or died without trace in the war. Madli never speculated about his fate, though once she told me she'd do anything to have him alive. Again, in a strange mood, she said she felt they would be together soon. A premonition of death, do you think...?"

His brow furrowed, he began to pace a few steps back and forth. "She was shattered by the sight of death. One night we saw a woman killed by a bus. It slammed her broken body into the gutter. Horrible, and for hours Madli was drained of spirit. I could do little more than hold her hand till she returned from wherever she'd gone. Now that I've learned of her beating and rape and the murder of her mother by Russian soldiers I realise where her tortured thoughts had taken her, and understand the depth of certain longings."

He stopped pacing and looked across the room to where Carl picked at the pilaff remains and watched impassively. "Carl said Madli didn't belong to one man. He's right of course. Not the Madli we knew. I was reminded again at last spring's annual booze-up on the British embassy lawn to celebrate my queen's birthday. Paddi wouldn't come. She was down with 'heat prostration', as she calls it. I was delighted. I was free to take Madli.

"If you were there you'll remember her stunning appearance in a strapless mini cocktail dress. Rather like the one she's in now, wasn't it? But in a deep blue that matched her eyes and set off the mantle of golden hair on her tanned shoulders. She snapped the ambassador's receiving line out of its usual alcoholic daze, I don't mind telling you. And her beauty and charm, under the crimson blooms of a flame tree, dazzled every man on that packed lawn. Several ignored their own women to have a word with her, or simply be near her. Their attention amused and pleased her, and I stood back, out of the picture for the moment. I wasn't put out. From early on I accepted her as she was, content to have her to myself whenever I could. Yet always afraid it would end too soon. And so it has..."

His gaze wandered beyond the room, his eyes wide and searching. "How long will we remember her? A few years? A few months? A few weeks? I don't think I shall ever forget her. And what is there to keep me here now? My Seato tour is nearly up. When it is I can return to England. Back there, amid pretence, inhibitions and furtive lives, I would have Paddi, knocked out by sleeping pills at night to avoid me, and one day, when I'm no longer a soldier, a job with her father's building firm in Guildford. That's where it began for us..."

He shuddered, then slowly brightened a little. "Or shall I stay on? Surely there's something I can do here. Teach, like Susan, for instance. And why not? Others have stayed. Look at Jock, that toothless, obese, happy-go-lucky Scot, sprawled half-dressed and unshaven on a rattan couch in a rundown old house on Suriwong Road while his cheerful Thai wife sells eggs and poultry from a fridge in their front room. Peter, once a top New York photographer, happily submerged in Samsaen with a jolly fat woman and a raft of kids, and hearing not a word of English for days on end. And Tony, poor Tony. A wonderful teacher, a drunken has-been, and a dreadful bore. Here for half a lifetime after he lost his school in Winchester for meddling with his students, and dead for a fortnight before any of us heard he was gone. That's anonymity, I suppose. A state I might prefer after this..."

Sighing profoundly, he ran his fingers through his short brown hair, lost in thought for a while; then again he stepped to the side of the sofa, and glanced round in surprise.

"Well, you have let me go on a bit, haven't you? Seems I caught you all in a reflective mood and quite willing to surrender the floor. I certainly rambled, but I'm sure you noticed that I didn't touch on Madli's murder. So here goes. We know the house was thoroughly locked and there was no forced entry, the gun that probably killed her is missing, and anybody with a key or access to a key could have done it. But we have no idea why she was killed, and if Somsak knew that he might find it easier to zero in on the murderer. Well, there's a likely reason behind my suspicion. Oh yes," he said, noting a sudden interest. "I have a suspicion, and it's getting stronger. I see a thread running through our stories that could pull together a credible background to her murder. It has to do with something that gave Madli and me a good laugh some weeks ago. But until I'm sure, I'm afraid I must leave you tantalised. Sorry, Somsak."

Moving to the front of the sofa, he held his glass on high and lowered himself to the floor by Susan's legs; he drained the glass and pondered a sliver of ice on the bottom.

"I have a strange impulse," he said quietly. "I would much rather confess to this crime than give Somsak my alibi, an alibi he can confirm, I'm sorry to say. When our beautiful and loving Madli was dying, I was at home in bed with my bloody wife."

Chapter Thirteen

Carl returned from the kitchen with the ice bucket and made room for it among the ashtrays and bottles of liquor and mix on the long centre table.

"There ya' are, boys and girls," he said expansively, rubbing his beefy hands together. "Now we can rev 'er up on that second wind we got while Ward was runnin' off at the mouth. Go easy on the ice, though. There ain't much. Mosta' the trays were left outa' the fridge, and we know who was the last iceman, don't we, Jimmy boy?"

"You making a federal case out of it, for Christ's sake?" Jim muttered, flipping over pages of the magazine yet again.

"Touchy, touchy. What you need is a good piece..." He leered at Maria; she quickly averted her eyes and he chuckled. "Not tonight, eh, Josephine?" He poured Scotch into his glass and popped in two ice cubes. "These little bastards are cold as poor old Madli. Sure hate to be where she is right now."

Jill scanned him scornfully. "The world would be a lot better off if you'd switch places with her."

He laughed and sidled over to the buffet, leaning back on it in his familiar stance. "No thanks, spook. I wouldn't even *join* her in the condition she's in."

"Did she bring out the best or the worst in people?" Betty wondered.

"She brought out the best in me," said Paul, smiling faintly.

"And what we see is what she got, right?"

"Well, I've changed. For the worse, in some ways. You know why." He took a hurried drink and stared at the glass. "It was unbearable to see the woman I loved become as you all knew her."

"As you all knew her," she repeated sarcastically. "Is that why you want to pin her murder on one of us? And in spite of what you've heard tonight, does your twisted mind *still* believe - ?"

"Yes!" he answered sharply. "And we're getting somewhere. Ward now has a suspicion that he'll explain sooner or later. And Somsak is learning a great deal from his prime suspects."

"Not this prime suspect," Frank growled, slowly pushing himself to his feet, his back braced against the wall of the stair landing and Dang cradled in his arms; she murmured sleepily and wrapped her thin arms around his neck.

"Silent Sam speaks at last!" Jill crowed. "Where the hell you been, fella'?"

Moving carefully down the room, he stopped at the table and looked soberly down on Somsak. "Now hear this," he said evenly. "On the night Madli was killed, I was at one of our up-country bases debriefing Phantom jet pilots after their missions over 'Nam. I stayed in our quarters at Udorn and flew back to Bangkok in the morning. The United States Air Force is my witness. That's it. You'll get no more out of me."

Somsak smiled and bowed slightly, and Frank continued on to Wilma's bedroom; opening the door, he paused and looked enquiringly over his shoulder, catching Wilma's startled eye as she twisted round in her chair to see where he was bound.

"Why, yes," she murmured feebly, a little flustered. "Yes, of course, dear boy."

He pushed the door shut behind him with an elbow as Dang began to stir in his arms.

"First on the wet deck, Frank!" Carl bellowed. "Want to follow your Uncle Carl, Jim? Then Ward, Paul, Freddy -"

"I'd rather not, thank you," Freddy stammered.

Carl glowered. "Ya' turnin' down a good screw?"

"Well, it's such a beastly hour."

"The best time, for fuck's sake. Ya' jolt 'em wide awake with a good stiff -"

"That's our Frank!" Betty cut in loudly. "Brief and to the point!"

Jill shrugged. "Didn't expect much out of him."

"Nor I," said Wilma. "He's afraid that any talk about himself would bring up Jackie. He hasn't mentioned her since the day she flew home to the States to divorce him over his affair with Madli. He still loves her, poor boy."

"Them's the hazards of the game," Jill quipped. "But there ain't no shortage of players."

"Madli was like a drug with Frank. You boys know what I mean. It threatened all that he cherished but he couldn't stay away from her. They met at Pattaya too. By the pool at the Inn. And they were soon in the *farang* gossip mill, though they tried to keep it quiet by slipping away to the Thai navy's beach cottages at Saddahip on the Gulf. It was around the time we were building our base there for the B-52s that are bombing North Vietnam."

"Et tu, old chum?" Ward mused.

Betty glared at him. "You're maddening. Why so bloody mysterious? If you have a suspicion -"

"And that's all it is. A suspicion of a possible explanation for Madli's murder. I may be wrong. I hope I am."

"I hate riddles. I think you're just trying to -"

"Dang?!" Noi suddenly cried, sitting bolt upright and peering around in fright. "Wheah my fwend Dang?" she wailed.

"Relax," Jill soothed. "Your friend Dang go sleep bedroom her friend Frank."

She tried to pull Noi back into her lap, but the girl squirmed free and sat on her heels, shaking loose her long black hair; the tight white slacks had inched below her navel and the brief red blouse had wrinkled around her small breasts.

"Noi wewy tied. No can sleep. Too much yabba yabba."

"Liar!" Betty huffed. "She's been dead to the world for hours."

"Noi, my dear," said Wilma. "Lie down on one of the beds upstairs. It's quieter there and you'll sleep much better."

Noi beamed. "Hokay. Fank you. You wewy kind lady." Rising slowly to her feet, she yawned and stretched so that her breasts jutted and her firm round bottom arched; then she wilted. "Noi no have fwend come bedwoom." She pouted and gazed wistfully at Ward.

With a wily glance at Betty, he began to push himself off the floor.

"Mr. Ward has a previous engagement," she drawled.

He fell back. "Frightfully sorry, Noi. Completely forgot." He raised his eyebrows. "Previous engagement, Betty?"

Thrusting out her round breasts, she pouted and languorously appraised him through her long lashes.

He chuckled. "Careful, young lady. I can be seduced quite easily."

"So can I, kind sir," she whispered eagerly.

Noi looked to Jim, inching a slender foot in his direction; he jerked his leg away, his attention glued on the magazine. Now a roguish wink caught Freddy off guard; clutching his bottle, he rolled his eyes helplessly towards the slumbering Reverend Ralph. And when she tried to catch Paul's eye, he took a sudden interest in the label on his bottle.

"Jesus Christ!" Carl roared, slamming the buffet. "Ain't nobody gonna' screw this poor little girl?!" Hitching up his trousers under the flowered Hawaiian shirt, he jabbed a thumb at his thick chest. "Well, I sure as hell will!"

"You sure as hell won't!" Jill snarled. Then, quickly smiling softly on Noi, she said, "Go to bed, doll baby. Jill come soon. Jill Noi's friend. Like Noi ooooh too much. Make very good together, you'll see."

She patted Noi's behind, gently pushing her towards the stairs; but Noi resisted, appealing to Ward with a look of bewilderment.

"It's all right, dear girl," he assured her. "Go to bed. Everybody Noi's friend."

Slowly brightening, she sent her melting smile round the circle and glided lithely to the stairs, the tantalising dimples on the curve of her animated little bottom peeping over the wide black belt; halfway up she paused and grinned impishly through the rails: "Bye-bye, ewybody!"

"*Sawadee*, Noi!" Susan called, smiling and shaking her head. "Such children they are. Unaffected and trusting. Certain of endless good times from generous *farangs*. And hoping that someday a nice American soldier will set them up in a little house filled with love and PX goodies."

"And lead them to the altar," Betty added. "Dozens of Bangkok bar girls are housewives in America today."

"But many have their hearts broken by GIs who don't keep their promise to send for them after they're shipped home. The girl is soon back in the bars, the only sure way she knows of making a living. Yet somehow her trust and hopes survive. The bar girl I knew -"

"Fuck me!" Carl thundered. "Am I hearin' right? Is our proper little school-marm screwin' around with Bangkok hookers?!"

Colouring somewhat, she gradually sipped her drink. "Sorry. I guess we've heard enough about bar girls for one night."

"If you mean that lout's pornographic accounts," Jill agreed. "But we're curious about your dolly, Susan."

"Well, Sumalee didn't strike me as a bar girl when we met. As you know, I teach English at the Royal Thai Military Academy. Mine are the morning classes run by Jusmag for the bright officer cadets they have selected for more advanced training in the States. Jusmag pays fairly well, but to get by I must teach afternoon classes at the American University Alumni Association. One day Sumalee approached me outside AUA and asked me to help her get into a class. She was eighteen and quite pretty. Her English was like Noi's and she wanted to improve it so she could be a tourist guide. They get good tips and a commission on the customers they take to the shops. I told her AUA students must have the equivalent of a grade ten education in the US She was very disappointed. She'd had only six years of schooling. I suggested private lessons, but they're expensive compared with AUA's token charge, and she couldn't afford it. She said her widowed mother and younger sister lived up-country and needed most of the money she earned at the Dew Drop Inn -"

"Aha!" said Jill. "Then it dawned."

"Not really. I knew the Dew Drop as a restaurant near the Erawan Hotel but I'd never been there. Sumalee said she worked at night so I thought she was a waitress. I had no idea its character changed completely at night."

"In a flash," said Ward. "I once saw an American army major romancing an Air France stewardess in there over a candlelight and wine dinner. It was early and I was about the only other diner. Some time between the main dish and dessert, while they danced cheek to cheek to soft recorded music, the night people began to descend. Soon there was an explosive blast of Beatle rock and the poor devils and their table were swamped by a heaving mass of jiving Thai dollies and GIs and other *farang* men. They fled in terror. When Frank and I dropped in on our booze mission we found the usual deafening bedlam and throngs of Nois and Dangs."

Susan nodded. "That's how I found it. I'd decided to teach Sumalee for nothing in my noon hour. I went there around ten at night to tell her. The scene was astonishing, and when I finally picked her out in the crowd I knew she was part of it. Tight satin mini frock, crippling high heels and hair piled up. Just as Carl described his bar girls. It didn't matter. I wanted more than ever to help her. I grabbed her hand and took her outside. She was embarrassed to have me see her like this, but so happy when I told her I would teach her English every noon hour at her home..."

"That's unusual," said Betty. "*Farang* teachers I know make their private students come to their house."

"I can't. I share a rented house with three *farangs* and we've agreed not to teach at home because it can get out of hand. Anyway, Sumalee's place turned out to be a brief walk to my afternoon class at AUA. She had two small rooms above a barber shop in a congested neighbourhood opposite Lumpini Park. They were spotless. She had a flimsy dinette set, an old dressing-table and chest of drawers, a crude four-poster enclosed in a mosquito net, and a small metal Buddha in a glass case surrounded by joss-sticks and fresh flowers in plastic vases. She cooked our lunch on a charcoal pot on her narrow balcony, usually a Thai curry or a terribly hot shrimp soup. A pleasant hour for me. Sumalee's very bright. It's surprising how quickly her English improved."

"Many Thai do far better with our language than we do with theirs," Wilma sighed. "I'm quite hopeless."

"My Thai," Betty crowed, "is actually looking up."

"Well, as Sumalee progressed I raised her sights. I took her to see my Jusmag boss. He liked her. He said he would consider hiring her as an office receptionist if she acquired the appearance and poise for meeting and dealing with people. It meant grooming her for the job, and really, I'd be out of my depth. But I knew someone who could. Madli, of course. I had met her at *farang* parties and been most impressed. She radiated presence and poise. I decided to sound her out by phone. I got a gracious reception. Madli let me go on at length about Sumalee's situation, her hope of a better life, my attempts to help her, and the polish she desperately needed to qualify for that receptionist job at Jusmag. I said that only someone of her background could coach Sumalee in such things, and I begged her to take it on. Madli sounded quite intrigued, but she wanted time to think it over."

Glancing at Meg, yet attentive on her cushion, her expression unchanged, she smiled warmly. "Next day her mother phoned the Academy to tell me she'd do what she could for Sumalee. She even suggested that I take her spare bedroom for a spell so we might cooperate. I'd work on Sumalee's English at noon, Madli would take over after I left for my AUA class, and we'd compare notes later. I was elated. Sumalee more so, for Madli also paid her living expenses to keep her free of the bars while we prepared her. It went so well. Sumalee has a natural grace. In Madli's hands she soon had good taste in dress and make-up, a quiet self-assurance, and appealing manners. An extraordinary transformation. We were tickled pink as you can imagine. Sumalee easily got that receptionist job, and before long her ability won her a sensitive position as file clerk in Jusmag's planning department."

"Well, bully for you," said Betty. "But was that really our fun-loving Madli playing a selfless 'Enry 'Iggins to a bar girl's Eliza Doolittle? Bit out of character, I'd say."

"Very generous of her," Maria ventured, her sudden voice drawing an enquiring look from Jim; she avoided his eye, and in a moment he returned to his magazine.

"Indeed," said Susan. "She helped a poor country girl escape the bars to a decent life. Sumalee felt grateful and indebted. Madli's death must be a terrible shock. They had become close, though never again did they meet at Madli's."

"Madli was damn glad to get you out of there, I know," Jill said. "But what in the world did she do to make you kill her?"

Susan's serious blue eyes met her mocking gaze. "Really, Jill. I had no reason to kill her."

"She asked you to leave," said Wilma. "She wouldn't tell me why, but she appeared disturbed over something."

Jill nodded knowingly. "Still waters run deep. Was our quiet little Susan trying to steal one of Madli's boyfriends?" She glanced from Jim to Ward. "How about it, fellas?"

Ward shrugged. "Could have been any one of a dozen womanly reasons."

"It was my fault," said Susan. "Madli was worldly and travelled. I was an immature girl of twenty-five. That's how she described me when she told me to stop criticising the way she lived."

"You and Maria make a fine pair," Jill muttered.

"I told her she was hurting herself and her family. We argued. Quite strongly."

"She didn't like you spying on her."

Susan brushed a stray blonde hair from her brow and straightened the blue chiffon over her bare knees. "I lived there for a while. I got to know and love the children. I couldn't help but see what was going on. She led a perilously loose life. I felt I had to say something."

"I appreciate that, Susan," said Paul, raising his glass before downing the drink.

"And I appreciate you tucking into the booze," said Wilma. "Makes you much more agreeable, Paul. Though heaven knows you're far behind Freddy."

"He's what?" Freddy swung around and back again; spotting Paul, he frowned. "Somebody said you were..." He pointed over his shoulder with his bottle and it came to rest there at the slope. "Have you found your keys yet, old man?" he enquired earnestly.

"Good Lord!" Betty cried. "He's off on another cycle!"

"You have me confused with my recycled friend here," he slurred, poking his bottle at the Reverend Ralph's paunch; the Reverend let out a louder wheeze and slumped a little further in his chair.

"Please let me take him home," Beatrice begged, wringing her hands as she got to her feet.

"Stop leaping up like that," said Paul. "You'll wake up little Tim."

"What shall we do with this body?"

Freddy gave the Reverend's paunch another poke with his bottle.

"I want to take it home," Beatrice whimpered, sinking slowly onto her chair to up and down motions of Paul's hand.

"I think we all want a good strong coffee," said Betty, springing up from her cushion. "I'll make it. Some sandwiches too, though I demand help with them. Somsak!" He started and she laughed. "You just volunteered for kitchen police. Hop to it. Time you did something for your keep."

He stood up, looked around with a smile and a shrug, and followed her out the courtyard door and on to the kitchen.

Chapter Fourteen

Hands on her hips and her lips pursed, Betty surveyed Alun's kitchen, and shook her head in disgust. "Look at this mess! Jim and Carl slopped bits of fish and rice all over the table. And their dishes! Yuk! Really! Men are so untidy."

Somsak grinned. "My wife won't let me near her kitchen."

"Raiding the fridge is one of Western man's perks, but it never occurs to him to clean up afterwards." Piling the dishes in the sink, she dampened a dishrag under the hot water tap and plopped it on the table. "It's one more nasty job he leaves to women."

He stood back and watched her attack the table with the rag. "Miss Betty," he finally ventured. "How can I help? I'm lost..."

"Ah." Braking the rag in mid-swipe, and smiling at his sheepish expression, she pointed out the serving trays on a top shelf. "Get a couple of those down, Somsak. On one you can put big platters for sandwiches and small bowls for pickles and such. On the other a bowl of sugar, jug of milk, coffee mugs, small plates, spoons and forks, paper napkins..."

"Good as done," he said briskly, reaching for the big trays, opening the glass door of the china cupboard, picking out the pieces they needed and setting them where they belonged. "My, but Mrs. Wilma has very nice china."

"Nice everything. She has good taste. So did Madli, and she didn't give a damn about the price either. There." She made a last swipe with the rag and tossed it in the sink. "A clean table for our own mess... Now where's the coffee? In the pantry?"

"Do you like our Chinese coffee?"

"Hardly. It's awfully bitter. I can drink it, but only with a lot of condensed milk." She opened the pantry door and gasped, "Good Lord! Wilma's got half the PX in here!"

He looked in and pointed to the cans of evaporated milk on a shelf. "Mrs. Wilma gave my wife all she needed of this for our last baby."

"I know her generosity. She showers me with PX wine, fags, coffee, cosmetics. She'd probably keep me in PX canned food if I asked. But I don't like to take advantage." She found coffee, bread, sandwich ingredients and relishes and they carried them to the table. "Somsak, I'll get the coffee going and you open the cans of salmon and tin of ham. There must be an opener in one of these drawers... Yes, here you are."

He forced the opener into a can of salmon while she ladled coffee into a large percolator, filled it with cold water, and put it on the stove. "Do you eat only *farang* food at home?" he asked.

"Heavens no! That's only for those with PX or commissary privileges. I can't afford the atrocious prices on imported foods in the shops." She laid rows of bread slices on the table and began spreading them with salmon or ham as he handed her opened cans. "No, Somsak. My girl, Sanguan, stretches my bahts in the open market by Klong Lawd. She buys your wonderful fruits and vegetables, lots of chicken and a wide variety of fish, and now and then a slab of buffalo meat that I pretend is Kobe steak. She's a good little cook. I have two gas rings but she does everything on charcoal pots."

"We have only charcoal pots. My wife works wonders on them."

"I admire most everything your women do, and what they've achieved."

"They've come a long way in a short time. Not so long ago they were simply 'the hind feet of the elephant', as Thai men described them. It was meant as a compliment."

"What an odd way to put it! I remember a description in the diary of an 18th century missionary that my newspaper published. He mentioned the 'humble and obedient Siamese women who kept busy around the house while their lord and master slept and played.' Those were the days, my friend."

He chuckled. "Yes. Now our women own hotels, cinemas, supermarkets, factories, bus lines. They run banks and large companies. They're doctors, lawyers, teachers, engineers, architects. They pursue a high education at home and abroad to help their country develop. And they win international beauty contests, don't forget. We have many beautiful women."

"Do you begrudge your women their freedom?"

"On the contrary, because they don't abuse it. They master jobs in many fields but they still consider man superior."

"Do they, now? Or is that a clever ruse to disarm you while they slowly take over this male stronghold...? Blast! I forgot to light the gas under the coffee. There. It won't take long."

"No, Miss Betty. Thai women are content to be man's creatures, feminine and subordinate. Obedient to the rules of man, her master."

She abruptly turned to face him. "Then what must you think of us?"

"You...?"

"*Farang* women. We recognise no rules or master. We flaunt our freedom and equality. Your wives wouldn't think of going alone to nightclubs, bars, house parties and hotel swimming pools, or date another woman's husband. Your daughters wouldn't dare sashay around Bangkok in skin-tight micro skirts and shorts as American teenagers do. We're shameless. Our conduct insults your customs and propriety. Surely our presence concerns you."

He shrugged helplessly. "Westerners have established their own society in my country, I'm afraid. And our worst elements provide vice of every kind for their amusement. The behaviour shocks. It's foreign to everything decent and sacred here. Our concern is to preserve all we can of Thai society. *Farang* women should be the concern of *farang* men."

"*Farang* men!" she snorted. "We're all tarred with the same brush, for heaven's sake. Nothing's sacred. Our senseless pursuit of pleasure would embarrass anybody of sound mind. And you'll see, Somsak. A few awkward days of grief over Madli and this lot will be back with the whole jolly cast in its endless farce. Boozy parties, alcoholic nightmares, carefree games of musical beds. It's a wonder we don't have a great many crimes of passion."

He smiled. "We have enough crimes of passion of our own."

"And damn entertaining they are, too. A few days ago our front page had a large picture of a weeping woman pointing a pistol to show a bunch of gawking reporters and cops how she killed her rival in love..." She caught her breath. "Somsak. Is this a woman's crime?"

"Mrs. Madli?"

"There are half a dozen women suspects."

"I don't know. Not yet."

"Okay. Now this may sound silly, but if you had reason to charge someone here with her murder, who would you prefer it to be?"

"Miss Betty. We mustn't -"

"Come on," she teased. "I won't tell a soul. Promise."

He hesitated, amused by her quizzical look. "All right then. Carl. I'd prefer it to be him."

"But he says his job lets him get away with murder here."

"An idle boast, I think. Our courts would certainly test it if we had the evidence to charge him. If we had only a strong suspicion of his guilt we'd have him kicked out of the country."

"Would the CIA stand for that?"

"There's a way to beat them. We'd threaten to leak information to the media about Unistates Air's covert operations throughout Southeast Asia unless Carl was sent home. The US ambassador would see to it. That's how we got rid of one of Carl's fellow pilots we suspected of smuggling opium from Laos to heroin gangs in Bangkok."

"Very clever," she said approvingly, looking at him closely. "You don't like Carl, do you, Somsak?"

"Nor his kind," he replied. "We put up with a great deal from them for the sake of accord with our American ally. We have no say in what they do here and so..." He shook off the thought. "Anyway, Miss Betty, it's wishful thinking. Carl probably told the truth about his relations with Mrs. Madli and where he was when she was killed."

"I suppose he hasn't the guile to lie convincingly. Have you felt that others were lying?"

"I felt that some were a little careless with the truth, shall we say?"

"And Ward's suspicion? It bothers me."

He nodded. "And me. He says it has to do with a likely reason for her murder, and that a familiar thread in some of your stories is making it clear to him. Is he hinting that several of you have been up to something reckless, dangerous, illegal? Serious enough to cause murder, yet good for a laugh?"

"Bizarre, isn't it? Maybe Ward's just toying with a wild idea."

He sighed. "You might be right. But it's perplexing. We won't know what it's about till he tells us, and he'll tell us only if it amounts to anything. Not much help at the moment, is it? But you must have some thoughts, Miss Betty. I'd be interested in hearing them."

She shrugged. "For what it's worth, if you like. I think Carl's out, the big oaf. So is Frank. His painful loss of Jackie might be reason to kill the woman who caused it, but his alibi's airtight. Ward could have sneaked away from Paddi's side, killed Madli out of jealousy, and crept back to bed without her knowing. But he's not the jealous kind and I bet my life he wouldn't kill...

"We all heard Jim's cruel account of the alibi for Maria and himself. Ralph and Beatrice? A pitiful pair. I don't know why they're here. Wilma's alibi is soft but her motive's stale. She's used to Dick's philandering. Would she wait this long to get even with one of his women? I don't know, but the Italians say 'revenge is a dish that's best eaten cold'. At least she kept us entertained. Susan had to bore us with more guff about bar girls. Now that one's a puzzle. I remember Madli saying that a Canadian teacher persuaded her to help groom a Thai girl for a Jusmag job, and to let her take the spare room while they worked on the girl together. Madli didn't sound too keen about it, though she often had perverse versions of her relationship with people if they annoyed her, and Susan told us how she did just that. You must ask her where she was that night...

"And Jill and Freddy. Poor Freddy. Looks as though he wouldn't hurt a fly, doesn't he? Yet those are the sort who do. Jill? She'll play cat and mouse with you, Somsak, till she tires of the game, then tell you what she pleases. She has a temper, and it's no secret that she resented Madli having other lovers."

Then drawing herself up she said, "There you are, Somsak. Betty's capsule comment on the crime. And our super snack is almost ready to deliver."

Shutting off the gas under the boiling coffee, she started to stack sandwiches on the platters, and to put dills, pickled onions and relish in the small bowls. He sensed that she watched him from the corner of her eye.

"Phone your headquarters," she suggested. "Maybe the pistol's been found, or a likely accomplice picked up. You'd save a lot of tedious time with us if -"

"I would have been phoned right away if there had been any developments."

She glanced at him uncertainly. "Well..."

"Miss Betty. Did you not leave somebody out of your very interesting comment on the crime...?"

She grimaced. "I did. I left out me, of course." And desperately: "Somsak, I can't talk about me in front of those people."

"Is that why you...?"

"Yes. I thought if I got you on my own I might persuade you to go after Madli's killer without any more questionable help from us. Stupid of me, I realise. It's Paul who won't let us off the hook. He's so bloody certain her killer's in that room, and we try to dodge suspicion by telling all sorts of haphazard tales."

"Haphazard but revealing," he said. "So they could be valuable. And when Ward proposed this way of getting at the truth, you went along with it."

"Well, it sounded like a bit of fun. Tell a lot of rubbish about ourselves and Madli, toss in a likely alibi, have a good laugh. That's right up our alley. I'm sure nobody expected it would go this far. But after Paul dropped his surprise about the keys that made us the likeliest suspects, we seemed to shed all restraint. Some of it's harmless, even entertaining. But some is deadly serious or downright nasty. And it's not over yet, darn it."

"Believe me," he assured her. "I'd like to end this game and Miss Meg's ordeal, but it's out of my hands."

She pulled her long hair together at the nape with both hands and suddenly let it go. "Oh well. I guess I can tell my wretched little tale, as if anyone cares. At least it explains how I came to meet Madli. Four years ago I followed my journalist lover to Southeast Asia and he ditched me in Saigon for a Vietnamese bird. I was thousands of miles from home, penniless, heartbroken, and too ashamed to ask my told-you-so family in London for help. A nice Aussie saved me. He advised me to try for a proof-reader job at the Siam World in Bangkok. He said there were frequent openings because the English hippies the paper lured off the hashish trail to Vientiane never stayed long. He lent me the air fare and I arrived at the World the day one of them left. I started work right away. In a few months I became a reporter. I did well. A year later I was made social editor. When I heard of Madli's flair with fashions and sketching, I convinced my boss that she should do a page for our Sunday paper. I asked her by phone and she agreed. We hit it off. We became good friends. I was soon a familiar member of her crowd, though I did back off a bit from her wildest scenes..."

She looked at him appealingly. "There's nothing more to say about Madli and me. I liked her. I wouldn't harm her. But earlier on I said those hours in the witching time of night, the hours of her

death, are often difficult to account for. I can't account for mine in
there. Not in front of Ward."

"Ah," he said, "I suspected. You love him, don't you?"

She looked away, biting her lip. "I have done since the moment
Madli brought him into our circle two years ago. He had eyes only
for her, of course. But I knew she discarded her men in time. I
could wait. She kept him till the very end. Now it's my turn. He
knows me as a jolly, carefree young woman. I'm not known to sleep
around. He likes me. I'm sure he can love me. I want him to love
me. So much. I must not destroy this chance."

"I don't understand. How could you...?"

She turned to him intently. "Jim forced that alibi on Maria. It
was a lie but she really didn't deny it. For one of two reasons. She
needs the alibi because she killed Madli. Or she thinks he needs the
alibi because he killed Madli. Only Maria can tell you. I don't know
if Jim was being considerate of her, in spite of his cruelty. Or
considerate of me."

Nervously she began to rearrange the sandwiches on their platters
and to make room for the coffee pot on the tray of mugs and small
plates. He had to lean closer to hear when she spoke.

"I'm another Sharon, Somsak. A woman in need. A warm
blooded woman without a man because my heart is set on Ward and I
wanted him to see I had no attachment. But this is Bangkok, sensual
and cloying, as Jill said. And it had been a long time for me. Jim's a
machine, unloving and unlovable. He was after me for ages. A few
weeks ago I gave in. But I demanded absolute secrecy. He agreed.
He thought I was thinking of Maria. He didn't know my feelings for
Ward. It was a tidy arrangement, the sort he likes. Every Thursday
we went separately after midnight to one of those short-time hotels on
Petchburi Road. We left separately around three or four. That's
where we were when Madli was killed. Now do you see why I
can't?"

"I see no reason for you to worry. What you did was very human.
I'm sure Ward would understand."

She drew a tremulous breath. "I am not Madli. Very few women
have the power she had over men. They willingly shared her. They
lined up for her favours. Ward and Carl have told us it didn't cool
their passion. They were grateful for their portion. I don't have her
power of attraction. I'm afraid if Ward knew I've behaved like a little

animal he will see me as just another *farang* tramp, another round-heeled push-over. It's a womanly fear, Somsak. I can't get over it."

He nodded sympathetically. "Then we must see that he never knows."

"But how? Jill will be as merciless with me as she has been with others. She probably senses my feelings for Ward. She could accuse me of killing Madli so I can have him. You can imagine how that would titillate. It would certainly compromise Ward and me. And worse. If it made Jim think his phoney alibi for Maria could get me into trouble, he might blurt out the awful truth."

"The truth is what we're after," he reminded her kindly. "But Jim lied. Perhaps others did too. And Maria and Susan failed to mention where they were when Mrs. Madli was murdered. There is much to sort out and more to come. I believe your story, Miss Betty. In there you need only make up a credible account of your movements that night and I will divert attention before you can be accused or mocked."

"You would do this...?"

"Leave it to me."

"Oh, Somsak," she sighed. "I'd be so grateful. Such a relief, you have no idea..." And contritely, a hand on his arm: "I should have been straight with you from the start, shouldn't I? It's you who understands."

He shrugged and smiled. "I also understand that our friends wait impatiently for your strong coffee and grand snack." He pointed to the loaded trays. "Shall we - ?"

Suddenly her fingers clutched his arm and she whirled in shock towards the courtyard.

A piercing wail had cut through the air from the big room beyond.

Chapter Fifteen

"Don't touch him!" Beatrice moaned. "Go away! All of you!"
She sprawled across the still form of the Reverend Ralph, face
down as he was on the floor, one arm around his head, the other
trapped under his belly. Carl stood astride his legs, unconsciously
cracking his knuckles.

"My God!" cried Betty, bursting into the room ahead of Somsak
and looking fearfully about. "What happened?!"

Showing concern, Jim, Ward and Susan clustered by the odd
tableau, while Wilma and Maria leaned anxiously forward in their
seats, Freddy slouched indifferently in his and Jill stayed cool on hers.
Little Tim slept on, an arm around his school bag, his face buried in
his pillow; his father and sister seemed unmoved but Noi cowered in
fright by the lower stair landing. In the open doorway of Wilma's
bedroom, Frank calmly tucked his shirt into his khaki drills as Dang,
wide-eyed with alarm, clung to his arm with one hand and clutched a
sheet around her with the other.

"Tell us what happened!" Betty demanded, glaring accusingly at
Carl.

"It was so sudden," said Susan. "Ralph -"

"Leave him alone!" Beatrice sobbed.

"Not to worry, old girl," Freddy soothed. "I've known chaps to
sleep much better on the floor than in a feather -"

"Freddy! For Jesus' sake!" Betty stormed.

The Reverend grunted under Beatrice's weight and resumed his
whistling wheeze and sporadic snore.

Betty slumped. "I thought... Carl... Christ Almighty!"

"I see him start to slide off his chair," said Carl, moving away
from the Reverend. "I get behind him and take him under the arms to
pull him back. He slips so I grab his shirt. It rips wide open and he
sinks to the floor on his face."

"Then Beatrice throws herself across the room screaming her bloody head off," Jill said wearily.

"Ralph's back..." Wilma stammered.

"Poor man," said Susan.

"...covered with huge red welts," Wilma finished weakly.

"What...?" Maria tried.

"Hives," Freddy said knowingly.

"Whip welts more like it," said Jill. "Madli, I bet."

"Wicked, wicked woman!" Beatrice wailed.

A white, red and brown blur streaked down the room with long black hair flying and now Noi clung to Frank's other arm and exchanged a scared look with Dang across his broad chest.

"Come sit down, Beatrice," Susan said kindly, reaching for her hand to help her up. "We'll look after Ralph."

She resisted, her plumpness shaken by sobs. "I wanted to take him home. Paul wouldn't let me."

"Paul's got a lot to answer for," said Jill.

"How was I to know he was in that state?" he croaked.

"You didn't know your wife either, did you?" she taunted.

"Perhaps none of us did," Ward murmured.

"She and me just screwed, period," said Carl. "How about you, Jim?"

Jim caught Maria's blank gaze for a second and quickly looked away.

"I say," said Freddy amiably, pointing his bottle at the Reverend. "What shall we do with the body?"

"Get rid of it," said Frank; freeing himself from Noi and Dang, he gently raised Beatrice to her feet, hushing her weeping protest as he steered her to the sofa and sat her by Maria. "Take it easy, ma'am. We'll take care of your boy." He patted her shoulder and nodded to Carl; carefully turning the Reverend onto his bruised back, they lifted him by the legs and armpits and carried him into Wilma's bedroom with Noi and Dang hard on their heels.

"Don't hurt him," Beatrice whispered; Susan sat on the other side of her and she and Maria took her hands to calm her.

Dang was first out of the bedroom, clutching the sheet, her clothes and Noi. Frank followed Carl and closed the door behind him.

"Snug as a bug," he said, giving a thumbs up. "That guy could sleep through an earthquake." Then whacking Noi and Dang playfully on their bottoms, he pointed to the stairs. "Back to bed. Both of you."

Dang snuggled against him and looked up appealingly. "Fwank sleep me?" she asked wistfully.

"Fwank say go to bed!" he barked, raising his hand threateningly.

With frightened yelps they bounded across the room, and the bamboo chair by the landing snatched away Dang's billowing sheet so that she was just an exquisite brown body racing Noi up the stairs.

Frank chuckled. "Ain't she somethin'? That little doll would keep you in the sack for days, I swear." Filling a glass with neat Scotch, he sat on the bamboo chair that the Reverend Ralph had slept on for hours and looked round the circle. "Well now, you guys find your killer?"

"Just waiting for their signed confession," Jill drawled.

"Carl," said Betty. "Sorry about..."

"No sweat, babe. Carl's a lady killer. He don't clobber old men."

"There's coffee and sandwiches on trays in the kitchen. Would you and Jim...?"

Leaving their drinks, they disappeared into the courtyard. Meantime, Ward returned with his glass to his place on the floor by the sofa while Somsak again took his seat beside Maria. And when Carl and Jim brought in the loaded trays, Betty shifted bottles and ashtrays to make room on the table.

"Lord, I didn't realise I made so many sandwiches," she went on cheerfully, kneeling on a cushion to serve. "They're good, though. Only the best PX canned salmon and ham from Wilma's bountiful larder. Let's know if you want sugar or milk in your coffee."

Chattering away, she filled the mugs, added milk and sugar when called for, and passed them round with plates of sandwiches and pickles.

Meg glanced at her father; he nodded and she came to the table, taking back two sandwiches and coffees. As others tucked in with murmurs of appreciation, Freddy dismissed all offers with a casual wave of his bottle.

Somsak sat back with a black coffee and a cigarette, aware of subdued feelings, Betty's bid to enliven them with chit-chat, the half-hearted responses, and Jill's concentration: gripping her mug in both hands, she sipped the hot coffee and stared intensely at Beatrice.

And as if suddenly conscious of the expectancy around her, Beatrice carefully rested the coffee she had barely touched on the table, and pulled the red bandanna from her voluminous green frock. She mopped the perspiration on her plump cheeks and pudgy neck, then timidly, almost to herself:

"He's a good man, really. He works very hard for the church, helping the poor and the troubled and all. He's a good Christian. But weak, so very weak. He can't resist the flesh for long. Not always his fault, mind. Some women become infatuated with their church minister and make advances. It happened several times when he was younger, and he often yielded..."

Twisting the bandanna round her fingers, she squeezed her eyes shut for a moment. "Then for a long time it was young girls. Girls in Sunday school and youth clubs. Guides and Brownies. Some young girls tease old men like him. They lead them on for a lark. He couldn't keep his hands off them. Parents found out and reported him to church governors. One of the newspapers heard about it and -"

"I know the case," said Betty. "Though I think it was a different name -"

"We had to change our name."

"No matter. And the case wasn't much. There is always some church minister running off with a parish wife, or mucking about with choir boys or girl guides. What I remember is the front page of a New Zealand tabloid that was tacked up at my boyfriend's London newspaper as an example of a clever headline. A church minister had sued for slander when the tabloid claimed he touched up young girls in his congregation. But the paper had the goods on him, and when he realised it and dropped his suit, it gloated in huge type, and I quote: 'Go Unfrock Yourself, Reverend Twilling'. It was a riot."

"Go unfrock yourself," Carl slowly repeated, chuckling as the meaning became clear.

"Very clever," Wilma said faintly.

Beatrice winced. "It was dreadful. We were badly shaken. I had nowhere to turn. I have no relatives, no close friends, no one to confide in. And I am all he has. We've been married thirty years. I couldn't..." She shook her head. "In spite of everything I've never even thought of leaving him. We hid in the countryside for weeks. But we had no money, and Ralph can do no other work. We begged the church governors to give him something to do. They were understanding, and Ralph's been a long and faithful servant. They offered this mission and suggested we use another name so we might bury the past."

Smiling faintly, she glanced shyly at those near her. "It's five years now, happy years mostly. We like the country and we get along well with its people, though we've had disappointments. Thai Buddhists and Muslims are difficult to change. We've converted only one to Christianity..."

"Don't feel badly," said Susan. "In the last century, an American missionary named Bradley converted only six Thai in thirty-five years."

"...and we've persuaded very few *farangs* to come to church."

"Because you're so bloody stingy with the communion wine," Jill gibed.

"If *farangs* went to church," Susan said, "they'd have to listen to their conscience, and that would spoil their fun and games here."

"Good God!" Jill snorted. "No wonder Madli gave you the heave-ho."

Jim looked up from his coffee. "Did you know she met Ralph at one of our bases up-country? She was with me on a selling trip and he was trying to preach Christian morality to those wild young GIs. I remember Madli joking that he didn't have a hope in hell of getting them to quit whoring around."

"Ralph took me to see Madli," Beatrice said. "I rather liked her. We had tea and a nice chat. Later, when she was going away for two or three days, she asked us to stay with the children. We did so a few times after that, and we became quite close."

She looked fondly towards Tim, now covered by Paul's jacket, and Meg, who watched her calmly, then turned away with a little sigh. "I always wanted children of my own, but it was not God's will... Well, after our last stay with Meg and Tim a few weeks ago, Madli came to our compound and took Ralph off to one side. She appeared angry and contemptuous, and as she talked he became frightened and cowed, nodding all the while as though he agreed with everything she said. When she was gone I asked him what was wrong. He said it was not important, but I could see he was in a state and I worried. That night I awoke for some reason. Ralph was not in his bed. We had a new young servant girl and... Well, I got up and went outside to check on her quarters. I saw a faint light in our church. I crossed the compound to see if Ralph..."

She twisted the bandanna tighter now and shuddered. "The door was locked but I heard sounds, terrible sounds. I found a loose window shutter and looked in. Dear God. The light was from our church candles. Madli was in shorts and halter and he grovelled in his underpants at her feet. And she whipped him, furiously, her face twisted, her hair flying, her eyes like a mad woman's. All the while snarling 'beast, rapist, pig, child molester'. He moaned and kept repeating 'yes, yes, yes'. I couldn't bear it. I was terrified. I stumbled back to bed and waited in the dark. It was half and hour before he came to his bed, limping and groaning. I went to him and held his hand. I told him I had seen everything. I cried. He implored me never to say a word about it to anybody, ever..."

She looked around beseechingly. "You saw his back. It was worse that night. Awful welts and bruises. And blood. I bathed him. He finally fell asleep and I prayed it would not happen again. But it did, twice more, the last ten days ago. And it might have continued if she hadn't..." She stared at her hands, her voice falling away. "Monstrous sacrilege, yet each time I was drawn to that window as if I had no will of my own. It was like he was a pitiful slave, and she his evil mistress. And all so eerie in the flickering light of our church candles. Hideous punishment, but he seemed to accept it. Why? Was it - ?"

"His thing?" Jill suggested dryly.

Her plump chin dropped and again she wrung the bandanna. "I will never understand it. What came over Madli? Had she discovered our secret? Was she avenging those young girls in New Zealand...?"

"No," Meg said suddenly. "Mother found out that Uncle Ralph had tried to touch me."

"You again, kid?!" Jill snarled.

Beatrice buried her face in the bandanna. "Not Meg!" she sobbed. "Oh, please God, not Meg..."

Paul put a hand on his daughter's shoulder. "Madli was not much older than Meg," he said emotionally, "when she was beaten and raped by Russian soldiers. Think about it!"

"Dirty bloody Russians!" Freddy blustered.

"What did you do with the pistol, Beatrice?" Jill asked matter-of-factly.

Her head jerked up, her plump cheeks streaked with tears once more. "No. Oh no, I couldn't." She turned with alarm to Somsak. "I would never dream... I prayed that I could stop hating her. It's not Christian. But I'd never -"

"Hardly ever, you mean," Jill said. "Why didn't you tell Madli to stop whipping the hell out of your old lecher?"

"I was afraid of her."

"But not too afraid to stop her with a bullet, right?"

"I was home in bed when she died! Ralph was asleep in the same room!"

"And he'd sleep through an earthquake, as Frank said. You slip out, kill Madli with her own pistol, chuck it in a *klong* somewhere, and you're back in bed before the Lord knew you'd gone."

"What a terrible thing to say!" Beatrice protested, her voice trembling.

"It's all right, Beatrice," said Susan, taking her hand. "It's Jill's way. She doesn't mean -"

"I sure as hell do!" Jill snapped. "She'd do anything to protect that dirty old man of hers. She -"

"And speak of the devil..." said Betty as the bedroom door swung open and the Reverend Ralph leaned groggily against the door frame, mouth agape and drooling, pale rheumy eyes bloodshot, sparse grey hair tangled and on end; he'd draped a pink frock of Wilma's over his bare back and his trousers seemed in danger of falling.

"Beatrice?" he whined. "I want to be in my own bed."

"There you are," Freddy huffed. "Woke up he did because feather beds don't suit Uncle Ralph."

Beatrice heaved herself from the sofa and moved to her husband's side. Throwing off the pink frock, she hitched up his trousers and tightened the belt, wiped his drool, tidied his hair with her fingers, and took his blazer from the back of the bamboo chair and helped him into it.

All the while he smiled lopsidedly on the room. "Lovely party. Jolly fine company. Delicious dinner. Nice drinks. Enjoyed every minute. Thank you." The smile slowly faded and he looked pained. "Yet I must say I feel like I've been through the wringer. Head hurts. Back hurts. Nose hurts. Beatrice...?" She took his arm and he leaned on her.

"I'm taking him home, Paul," she said firmly.

He dismissed her with a wave of his hand.

"I'll drive them," said Jim, looking expectantly to Maria; she toyed with her cup, watching the milky coffee ebb from side to side. "And I might as well get in a swim and breakfast before I come back."

He followed Beatrice and the Reverend to the front door; as they put on their shoes, he again looked to Maria. "Anyone else for a lift?" he asked anxiously. She kept her eyes on her cup, and after a moment he opened the door and took the Reverend's arm to help him down the path to the gate.

"See you all in church!" the Reverend's quavering call came back.

Beatrice paused at the door, her eyes puffy and shimmery, her mousy hair straggly, and the sweat stains on the green frock wider now at her armpits and below her heavy breasts.

"I'm sorry," she said sadly. "I didn't want anyone to know, but you saw what she did to him so I had to tell of the terrible things I witnessed. I beg you not to let it go any further. We have nowhere else to go." She swallowed hard. "It's always been difficult, and there's no end to it. I don't know where I failed for him to become like this." She turned to Meg. "Forgive him, dear child," she whispered. Stepping outside, she carefully closed the door behind her.

"*Sawadee*, Beatrice!" Wilma called; and glancing round the diminished circle, she sighed. "Poor souls. What will become of them, do you think?"

They listened in silence to the fading roar of Jim's Mercedes in the dim early light.

Chapter Sixteen

Jill slowly uncoiled from her cushion by Wilma, balancing on her bare toes and pressing her long, slender hands against her trim hips. Head thrown back, she stretched voluptuously till her breasts seemed to swell in the orange jacket. For a moment she remained so, peering disdainfully down on the silent company, then collapsed in derisive laughter.

"What the hell's come over you? Am I to gather from these weird bloody looks that you feel sorry for our flabby, futile Beatrice and her ugly life with repulsive old Ralph?" She snorted. "Don't bother. She's a stupid bitch. She wonders where she failed him. The answer's right under her ass. In bed, of course. That's where men and women fail one another, though few admit it. And she's like submissive women everywhere. Heartless men treat them as rubbish and they haven't the guts to fly the coop!"

Smiling sardonically, she rubbed her hands, the fingers laced. "Beatrice and her Christian crap. Her whining prayers couldn't stop the devil in Madli, could they? And she's too dumb to see that the whippings reveal what comes over people. Passions, longings, lusts. They won't be denied. Madli was killing two birds with one stone when she punished that dirty old lecher for pawing young girls. Those whippings don't surprise me. Nothing I've heard this night surprises me. I know my Madli. And I know you lot. Your mood's not in keeping with the way we are. Snap out of it!"

Swinging a bottle of Scotch off the table, she held it to the light from a ceiling lamp. "Ah, forever amber," she crooned. "I like to dye Thai silk this colour. Such richness." Topping up the glasses within reach, she glanced round. "If somebody made more coffee we could have coffee royals. A grand way to greet the dawn. It's almost here, my friends. Darkness leaves but our mystery stays." For a second she stopped pouring to peer suspiciously at Betty. "Now what do you suppose our Betty was up to in the kitchen with Charley

Chan...? Snitching on our little white lies...? Bribing him to let her off the hook...? Never fear. She'll not get away with this depraved crime. Eh, Somsak?"

Catching Betty's eye, he was about to deflect Jill's thrust when she suddenly chortled and pointed at Ward. "Look! At last a breakthrough. He smiles! Cor blimey! as your ambassador might say." Now more genial, she stood the whisky on the table and picked up the gin. "A dash of mother's ruin for Wilma and Freddy."

"I shall help myself, thank you," he said. Struggling to his feet, he carefully proceeded to the liquor case by the buffet, groped inside and produced a bottle of gin on the first try; now swirling his free hand in the ice bucket near Betty, he frowned. "Blast. Nothing but beastly water. Not to worry, old man. Warm gin's quite acceptable on chilly nights."

Cradling the bottle in his arms, he weaved his way to Wilma's open bedroom, paused, and squinted over his shoulder. "Drink up, chaps. No reason to pack it in because Freddy's off to bed. Seems we're taking turns in here. Might as well be next." The door closed on his thin, rumpled figure, and immediately opened a crack on a hazy brown eye. "Don't go 'way, Somsak. Must confess to something or other. Slipped my mind for the moment." The door inched shut.

Frank chuckled wickedly. "What say we sneak Noi into the bed bare assed?"

"Balls," Carl grunted. "He wouldn't know what to do with her, for fuck's sake!"

"Here's Freddy's mistress," said Wilma, raising the gin and tonic that Jill had fixed for her. "He desires no other."

"And a fine mistress she is," said Ward. "Freddy could never stomach our ridiculous Seato command without her, I'm afraid."

"He can drink most of us under the table," said Jill. "Look what happened to Ralph when he tried to keep up with him."

"That queer old bastard," Betty sniffed. "Flagellation turns him on. He enjoyed Madli's punishment. But it made Beatrice hate her. She saw Madli as a devil's disciple. Maybe she felt it was her duty to kill her. As Jill said, she could easily slip away and do it without waking her sleeping lecher."

"Could someone else have stolen away from a sleeping partner to kill Madli?" Maria wondered, staring pensively at her glass.

"As easily as Beatrice," said Ward, smiling slightly.

"Surely they'd have to have a motive as good as hers," Betty said, her eyes darting from Ward to Somsak as she reached for a cigarette.

"No shortage of motives," Wilma sighed. "Jealousy, revenge, plain hatred. God knows we've raised enough doubts and suspicions to go round. Did any of us think our little game would come to this?"

"A Pandora's box we might have kept closed," said Susan.

"You got your job cut out, fella'," said Frank, peering sidelong at Somsak. "Only me and Paul have airtight alibis - him in Saigon and me a coupla' hundred miles north when she was killed." He grinned at the others. "Carve yourselves up, folks."

"Let's not forget Freddy," said Betty, lighting her cigarette. "His sort are hard to read. Maybe he's not the harmless buffoon he appears to be."

"Good point," Paul said. "I felt Freddy was trying to distract us, put us off guard, a while ago. Too bad you missed it, Somsak."

He shrugged. "It couldn't be helped. Miss Betty needed me in the kitchen."

"And Freddy," said Ward, "took us by surprise. Susan had wished that Madli's children had not seen so much life in the raw in their tender years. That set him off. He said he was an only child, and shielded from everything cruel and crude throughout his early years. He spoke lovingly of a very protective mother, and rather warily of a very strict father, a wealthy diplomat. After a private schooling in Melbourne, he went on to Oxford for a degree in something or other, then came home to work on a Canberra newspaper. His father rescued Freddy from that lowly job by wangling him this public relations position with Seato."

"I thought so," said Betty. "Many soft jobs with Seato and United Nations offices in Bangkok are wangled."

Ward grinned. "Except mine, of course... In brief, we also got an hilarious account of his disastrous marriage to a large and domineering woman, if you can imagine, a touching description of the young daughter he misses so much, and lyrical reasons for his passion for London where his father was posted for some years. In spite of all that gin he was quite lucid. Paul felt he was trying to put us off guard. I think he was trying to get us to see him in a good light. Integrity in his job and so forth. Yet somehow he confirmed my nagging suspicion about a connecting thread of circumstance behind Madli's murder..."

"You and your bloody thread of circumstance!" Betty complained, grinding her cigarette in an ashtray. "Why must you keep us dangling like this, for heaven's sake?"

He grinned sheepishly. "Sorry, old thing. Won't mention it again unless I'm sure there's something to it." And to Somsak: "In case you're wondering, Freddy didn't say where he was when Madli was killed. He had just brought her into his tale when Ralph began his amusing slow-motion slide off the chair, Carl tried to rescue him, the shirt ripped to reveal those ugly whip marks, and Beatrice went off her head."

"Freddy adored Madli," said Jill. "He'd do anything for her. She understood him. She listened to all his grief over his job and personal life, and helped him find what he needed when she realised he was homosexual. It surfaced in Bangkok like it has with others. But he's discreet. Not like those queens with their club behind the Europa Hotel on New Road. Funny lot, aren't they? It's surprising how many work for the *farang* newspapers here. Harry, Alan, Berry, John, Ali, to name only those I know. Our crowd has its share, of course, and some flaunt it all over town. I've seen that New Yorker with the haberdashery in Gaysorn, Jack what's-his-name, trying to pick up young waiters in the Erawan Hotel."

"The Thai despise that sort of brazen homosexual," Susan said, glancing at Somsak. "They corrupt many young people here. Yet Thais are tolerant of sexual tastes, unlike our hypocritical societies in the West. Bangkok's a haven for foreign gays of both sexes. I know of a popular British novelist who secludes himself in the Oriental Hotel on regular trips to find -"

"Jesus!" Carl exploded. "Listen to this prissy little school-marm, will ya'? First she gives us the low-down on fuckin' bar girls. Now she dumps all this crap about queers on us. What the hell you teachin' those poor young army officers, anyway? How to screw their way round the country?"

Susan blushed. "They're observations, that's all," she replied evenly. "One can't help notice what goes on in Bangkok. Everything, good and bad, is obvious."

"She's right," said Jill approvingly. With a fresh drink she moved to the bamboo chair near Paul and the children that Beatrice had occupied; turning it around, she straddled it, resting her arms on the back. She drank, and grimaced. "Warm Scotch. No worse than warm gin, I guess. Some say that's the way it should be drunk. There must be ice in the fridge by now, though." She looked about her. "No volunteers? Never mind. I'll go myself after this."

Swirling the liquor round the glass, she stared at it reflectively. "Reborn in Bangkok... Freddy was. Scores of others too. Not by some phoney belief. By chance. We stumbled onto this paradise while fleeing our painful hidden lives in hidebound holes. No need now to slink in search of the way we love. Here we bloom and ripen in the open. Forbidden fruit, my eye! Gorge yourself. It's a feast fit for a queen!"

She smiled, sipped her Scotch, and closed her eyes for a moment. "Oh, yes," she breathed. "The delicate, sensual excitement of our domain. It saves the sanity of many *farang* women here, I'll have you know. Women who wasted precious years on dreadful, faithless husbands and mindless studs before yielding to a natural longing in every woman. Some must be enticed, but once they become aware of one another they're in a whole new world. They know. Instinctively...

"Madli and I knew the moment our eyes met and our hands touched. The feelings she never realised she possessed were awakened by the Polish girl in London. And theirs was a hungry passion. They were together every moment they could steal till the day Paul took Madli to Saigon. That was it. No letters or phone calls to prolong the hurt. Thankfully, what she missed and craved she found in me. She wouldn't renounce men, yet I'm sure she preferred our love." And glancing at Ward, Frank and Carl: "You must remember the nights when we hung around after one of her parties while she decided who would stay. As often as not it was Jill, wasn't it...?"

"Right out of Zola," said Ward. "Nana was her name."

She nodded. "Though Nana was a whore, an expensive plaything of boring men of wealth and position. When she fancied a change she picked up one of her own kind off the street, cleaned and dolled her up, and put her at the head of the queue at times. But Madli -"

"Her passions demanded every experience as well."

"How could you tell what fires consumed her? It was impossible to know everything about Madli. She saw to that. I was content with our love. And there was more. We were artists. We sketched, painted, invented and shaped with silk, cotton, raffia, fishnets, canvas, anything. We were inspired. Our ideas came out of the blue. In the streets, markets, gardens, temples. By the sea and rivers and *klongs*. I wanted us to design Thai textiles. Together we had the flair and imagination to challenge the big firms, Design Thai and Star of Siam. She'd have independence and freedom. She was ready for it, but she wouldn't -"

"Too many irons in the fire," said Wilma. "Always flitting about here and there. Elusive as a moonbeam, much of the time."

"Best God damn handful once you caught her," Frank murmured.

"And doesn't Jill sound like her killer?" Betty offered brightly. "She who tried to nail a dumpy old Christian to the cross for the murder. Not to mention a promiscuous servant, a poor injured husband, a womanising booze salesman, a harmless school-marm, and a perfectly innocent social editor.. Jill bumped off Madli because she wouldn't play house with her. A worthy motive, don't you think?"

"As worthy as yours, Betty," was her wry retort; when Betty looked away she grinned. "Relax. Your secret's safe with me... Sure, Madli and I disagreed now and then. About children for one thing. I have none, thank Christ. She never tired of hers and that grated. About fathers. She worshipped hers, wherever he is. Mine..." Her eyes narrowed. "I despised the bastard. Vicious white trash he was. Beating my poor, ignorant black mother in drunken rages and for no reason. Killing her with his fists finally. It was escape for her but not for me. I was twelve and already a woman. His brutal bloody handiwork and he kept it up. Then one day, far out on our own in Montego Bay, he fell off our fishing boat and became tangled in the nets. He struggled, screaming for help. A rope's throw away and I let him drown, laughing insanely as he went under. I swore no other man would touch me and none has. My mother's sister, a harlot, put me through school and art classes. I was on the right track, thanks to her. The rest I did by myself. The beauty of Thai silk brought me here. I worked hard. I made it. My creations in Thai silks and cottons are in smart shops everywhere, here and abroad."

"This is one of them," said Maria shyly, caressing her rich suit of black silk. "We all have something of yours, I imagine."

"Several," said Wilma, glancing at Betty's yellow cotton frock and her own dressing-gown of blue silk.

"Not me," Susan said apologetically. "I'm afraid I can't afford you, Jill."

"Say no more, Susan. I shall whip up something nice to suit your pocket. Can't have you on the loose without my trade mark. In my game your prices rise with your reputation, and mine is up there with the best. How much better it would be if Madli had shared it." Once more she gazed on the amber liquid in her glass. "I loved her," she whispered achingly. "Oh how I loved my Madli. Her very last afternoon was mine. Mine alone to cherish forever. And as always, everything so beautiful. The scent of flowers and of one another. Our warmth on her cool sheets. Our touches, our cries..."

For an instant she pressed a hand to her lips, then let it drop to her breast. "I knew where she kept that little pistol," she said blankly. "I wonder. Did I return that night to release her once and for all from the filthy paws of rotten bloody men...?"

Her breathing quickened. "The thought of any man poking my sweet Madli made my blood boil!" she spat. "Yet I swore to bear it once in a while if we could be together, just us, just Madli and Jill. But she wouldn't -" Rapidly her face contorted as she gazed hatefully down on Meg and Tim. "She wouldn't leave her God damn brood, for Christ's sake!"

An unconscious reflex jerked the hand with the glass sharply towards them, and whisky splashed over the rim and onto the face of little Tim. He awoke with a loud cry and sat up, sobbing and rubbing his eyes. Letting go of the glass, she clapped her hands over her ears and ground her forehead against the back of the chair.

"Of all the lousy...!" Paul got out before Meg silenced him with a finger to her lips as she got to her knees and drew Tim to her; pulling a handkerchief from her skirt pocket, she mopped his damp face and neck and tried to soothe him.

Now Susan, quickly rising from the sofa and moving to Meg's side, lifted Tim into her arms and quietened his sobs. "There, there, little man. It's all right. You're okay. - I can look after him, Meg. - We're old pals, aren't we, Tim? Used to call on the hippo in the zoo, we did. And catch frogs and fish in the *klong*. - The hanky, Meg. - There. Blow the old nose real good, that's a fine fellow."

And sternly to his father: "Really, Paul. Why you had to keep this little guy around all night is beyond me. It's downright thoughtless."

"The boy was asleep," he replied lamely.

"Maybe so, but I'm going to put him in Wilma's small bedroom upstairs where he should have been hours ago. Don't get up, Meg. I can manage."

As she turned about, Tim squirmed in her arms, whimpered something, and pointed towards the floor. "Ah. The school bag. Mustn't forget Tim's school bag. - Thank you, Meg. - Here you are, little man. Hang on to it for all you're worth, and up we go."

Brushing her lips across a tear-stained cheek, she pressed his tousled dark head to her shoulder and started up the stairs. Halfway, the school bag slipped from Tim's light, sleepy grasp, glanced off a step, somersaulted through the iron railing, and landed at Jill's feet. The slight metal clasp gave way, the flap flew open, and the contents spilled out.

Meg started to get up to retrieve it, but sank back on her cushion when Jill clamped a foot on the satchel to prevent her.

Taking her eyes off Meg, she stared at it for a while; then, with her bare toes, she pushed aside the few small books and exercise pad, and, reaching down, seized the pistol by the butt.

Straightening, she pointed it down the room, and slowly swept it past the startled looks on Madli's friends till it was aimed at her daughter. Paul's arm went protectively around her and his face twisted with dread.

Meg's vacant blue eyes held Jill's ferocious glare. The arm trembled, the pistol shook, the voice cracked. "YOU! YOU LITTLE BITCH!"

Chapter Seventeen

"He was asleep again as soon as he hit the pillow," Susan said as she came down the stairs. "Poor little guy. He can't understand why we have his school bag. I promised he'd find it beside him when he woke up." She paused on the landing and looked towards the screen windows. "My gosh. Daylight already."

Once back in her place on the sofa, she again took Maria's hand and held it tightly. To her right, Somsak smoked and studied the small pistol on the table in front of him. Betty, one hip on her cushion and her legs stretched out, slumped over the table, head on her arms and eyes closed; and Wilma, gripping the arms of her chair, stared as though mesmerised at the paper-ball shade on a ceiling light.

By the buffet, Frank, Carl and Ward stood silently with their drinks, their attention on the side of the circle where Jill, arms crossed on the back of her chair and fingers dug into the sleeves of her orange jacket, kept a foot on Tim's satchel and a malevolent glare on Meg.

She leaned on her father's knee, one hand inside the open neck of her white school blouse, the other in her lap; her slender legs were drawn up under the blue-grey skirt, and her blank gaze lingered on the table where the pistol lay.

Ashen faced and eyes full of pain, Paul watched her, a hand straying in her long yellow hair; finally, he faced the others.

"This doesn't end our search for Madli's killer. I know my daughter. I don't believe for a moment what some of you might think. But only Meg can tell us why Tim's school bag hid the pistol that killed their mother. Only she knows the truth behind the purpose of this gathering. She arranged it."

"With your connivance, Paul," said Betty reprovingly.

"For good reason. When I got in from Saigon, and before Somsak had a word with me, Meg took me aside to tell me what she alone knew - her mother's pistol was missing, and each of you had a key to the house. And once Somsak had established that the house was carefully locked at bedtime and there was no sign of a break-in, she was sure that someone with a key came and murdered Madli with her own gun. It made sense. I wanted to confide in Somsak, but Meg said we'd have a better chance of catching the killer if we got you together, surprised you with what we knew about the keys and the pistol, and made you suspect that Madli's killer was among you. She felt it would bring out your relations with Madli and likely motives, and trip up the killer. It hasn't caught them. Not yet. But your attempts to clear yourselves of suspicion had you tearing into one another."

"Well done," Jill taunted, clapping her hands in slow rhythm. "You opened old wounds and inflicted a new batch. You wanted every one of us to pay for your wife's death to salve your insane jealousy and keep this little bitch above suspicion!"

"That's absolute rubbish!"

"Oh yeah? I think you were looking for a patsy. Plant the pistol on the most likely suspect to come out of this and your bloody daughter's in the clear. She hated us, and she hated to see her mother get more out of life than her airy fairy crap. She'd rather have her dead, for Christ's sake. Early on I said it's impossible to know what's behind those empty eyes. We do now. It's a heartless killer!"

"That's enough, Jill!" Wilma said sharply, pressing forward in her chair. "There's no call for more wild charges. We are all shaken by what we have seen. But let's be rational, for heaven's sake."

"Hear, hear," Betty murmured.

"Give Meg a chance," Maria pleaded.

"And don't interfere," said Ward. "Meg is Paul's child. She'll tell her father."

"Don't bet on it," Jill muttered.

"She will," said Paul, an anxious gaze on Meg as he waited.

It was a while before she turned away from the table where the pistol lay and looked into her father's eyes; and a moment longer before her small, flat voice silenced the unconscious sounds of the room:

"I lived every day in my mother, Daddy. She was so beautiful, so good and loving. We were happy in England, weren't we? But in Saigon everything changed. I didn't understand what was happening. First Uncle Dick and then other men. I never liked them. They didn't belong in our world. And when we had to move to Bangkok and leave you alone in Saigon, I began to feel that you had lost her. I became afraid for my mother. You weren't there to watch over her any more. So I did. Very closely. I think she sensed it. Sometimes, after she had behaved strangely, she would take me to her room and hold me and tell me again of the secret wonderland she and her father had found by the Baltic Sea. She knew the way and one day she would take me there. She asked me to be patient..."

She paused reflectively. "My room was up the hall from Mother's. At night I opened my door a crack and waited there on the floor in the dark so I would know if anyone came to her room. I never saw her visitors because my door opened the wrong way. But their voices told me who they were. It might be a friend she brought home if she had been out, or one of those with a key who had got in on their own and spoke when she opened her bedroom door to them. I sat by my door till they left. Then I went to bed. For a very long time I cried every night. But one night the tears wouldn't come. I could never cry again, ever. I stared at the darkness till I fell asleep. I always believed that some day my mother would be with me as she was when I was a little girl. She asked me to wait, so it must be true. But all these years it was like a huge balloon was blown up inside me. It hurt -"

"Enough bloody rubbish!" Jill snarled, slapping the back of the chair. "Tell us what you had to do with your mother's murder!"

"Why, you damn - !" Paul's heated protest began when Meg silenced him with a finger to his lips. "It's all right, Daddy. She wants to know how it happened. Everybody does..."

Slowly her gaze passed beyond Jill's angry glare as if drawn by memory. "Mother went to her room alone that night. I stayed by my door because sometimes her friends with keys came quite late. It was after one when I heard the lock on the front door click, and the door gradually open and close. They came up the stairs very quietly and tapped on Mother's door. It opened and I heard her say 'come, but don't expect me to change my mind'. Her visitor said nothing before her door closed, or when they left half an hour later, so I didn't know who it was. After a while, as I was about to shut my door and go to bed, mother began typing on that noisy old machine she got from the newspaper to do her fashion page. I wondered why she was doing it now. I sat on the floor and listened. The typing went on for an hour or more. When it stopped I waited a bit before getting up to close my door. Just then I heard a sudden bang. I couldn't think what it might be, but it seemed to come from Mother's room. I peeked round my door and down the hall. There was a light under her door. I had never gone to it to listen before. Now I did. There was not a sound. I held my breath, opened the door a little, and looked in..."

Now her distant gaze strayed to the pistol on the table, and the small voice softened till it was barely heard. "My mother lay on her side on the bed, her back to me, a sheet over her legs. She was very still. I went in, closed the door quietly, and tiptoed to the other side of the bed. She seemed to be staring at something far away, and to be in terrible pain. I saw where she was hurt, the wound in her breast. It was awful. For a while I couldn't move. Then I took the pistol from her hand and put it on the dresser. I sat beside her on the bed. I closed her eyes and kissed them. I brushed her hair until it shone like gold on the pillow. I held her hand. I talked to her. The big balloon inside me was going down. I felt lighter, almost peaceful, as though we were going to the wonderland she had promised, all of us as we were long ago..."

"Meg..." Paul began, his voice breaking; she turned to him, took his hand, and held it tightly.

"She left you a long letter, Daddy. That's what she was typing. I read it, so I know why she did this to herself. Her last visitor caused it. They were cruel. I promised her I would punish them, and I saw a way. I got Tim's school bag from his room, put the pistol and letter inside with his little books and scribbler, and left it on my bed. Then I sat by my mother and held her hand. When it was the time Alun got up and brought her coffee I kissed her, put out the light, closed her door, and went to my room."

Again she paused, remembering. "Poor Alun. She screamed when she saw Mother. I ran to her. She was sobbing with fright. I pulled her from the room, closed the door, and held her till she stopped trembling. I told her to phone Captain Somsak at home and get him to come quickly. I warned her not to say anything to anybody but him. Alun always does as I ask. And our Tim. Her screams had woke him up. He was at his door, whimpering and rubbing his eyes. I took him in my arms and told him our mother had gone in her sleep to a beautiful place far away and one day we would be with her again. He clung to me and cried. Our life here has always confused him, Daddy. Strange people around us, strange things going on. I knew how he felt. Our life in Saigon became just as bewildering to me... I gave Tim his school bag and told him he must keep it closed, guard it carefully, and say nothing about it to anyone.

"Then I phoned Aunt Wilma. She was nice to us and close to Mother. She came right away and went straight to her. I could hear her crying. She wanted to make the call to you in Saigon so I let her. As soon as you came I convinced you that Mother must have been shot with her own pistol by one of the friends who had a key to the house, and the killer could be found out if we got everyone together and showed that it had to be one of them. I was afraid if I told you the truth, as only I knew it from her letter, you might not want to expose the person who caused Mother to kill herself...

"It was someone with a key to our house, someone in this room tonight. But they were not to be found out. They were not to be shown up for the cruel thing they did. They took my mother from me. My dearest mother..."

"Meg, dear Meg..." came Paul's hoarse whisper. "I'm sorry... So very sorry for all you've gone through, all your hurt..." He swallowed. "And the letter, Meg...? You said..."

She nodded. "In Tim's school bag. Jill...? Please..."

Glaring suspiciously, Jill gripped the back of her chair, then grudgingly kicked the satchel across the floor to Paul's feet. Meg pulled it to her, reached inside, removed the little books, opened one, and took out the folded letter. Spreading out the many sheets, she passed them to her father, and watched as he scanned her mother's last words. There was a restless rustle of paper as he swiftly, intently, finished page after page...

Carl, Frank and Ward eyed him closely, their glasses poised. Betty sat upright and alert on her cushion. Maria nervously bit her lip and held fast to Susan's hand. Somsak stubbed out his cigarette and lit another. Wilma, her cheeks glistening with tears and her breathing tremulous, slumped on an arm of her chair and pressed a crumpled handkerchief to her mouth.

Then at last, Paul uttered a low moan, his hands fell to his lap, and he stared at Madli's letter, repeating weakly: "I can't believe it... I can't believe it..."

Now Ward, leaving his glass on the table, came and eased the letter from his limp fingers. "May I read it to everyone, Paul?" he asked kindly.

Looking bewildered, he peered at Ward as if unable to grasp what he meant; then realising, he appealed to Meg. "I don't know... Is it wise...?"

The thought had already occurred to her. "Why, yes, Daddy. Let everyone know. It may help them understand my mother. I did because I too have a love and a longing for someone that will never die."

Paul sighed. "Very well," he said submissively. "Read the letter, Ward."

He held up the pages. "Please," he said, glancing at the others in turn. "Not a word till I finish." And he began:

My dear Paul,

In a few minutes I shall take my life with the pistol you gave me in Saigon for my protection. It will need courage. I shrink from the slightest pain. I dare not think how I will look when I put the pistol to my breast and press the trigger. Yet I'm not afraid to die. I yearn for release, and the journey. I leave this letter because you deserve an explanation and my gratitude. It will hurt, but it's over now. Try to understand.

Soon after the war I became very intimate with a young Polish woman at the Middlesex Hospital in London. You met Sophia soon after you and I were together. She too was a refugee, one of many thousands of displaced persons. She told me little about herself, but I told her everything about my wonderful childhood in Estonia and the father I loved and missed so much, and my fear that he had died like my grandfather in the Russian advance near the end of the war.

One day, out of the blue, Sophia said she had information about my father but I must promise not to tell a soul. It was such a surprise, and naturally I agreed. She told me he was alive and in Moscow. I couldn't believe it, but she assured me it was true. She said I could talk with him on the phone, though it must be done in secret from an east European embassy in Paris. By now I suspected that Sophia worked for the Russians. It didn't matter. I was so excited at the prospect of talking with my father.

We got time off work to have a long holiday weekend in Paris as many Britons do. And there, at the Czech embassy, I was put through to Father. We cried and poured out our joy at finding one another. He had given me up for dead as well. I told him mother had been killed in our escape. I said nothing of our beating and rape by Russian soldiers. I said I was well and had a good job in London. He told me he was teaching physics at a university as he had done at home, but restrictions prevented him from saying more. I realised he was a prisoner.

Later, I asked Sophia if I could go to him. She said that would not be possible for now, but some day, when Russia no longer needed his special knowledge, they would let us be together. That was to be my enduring dream over the years to come. But Sophia said there were conditions for his well-being and survival. I must work for Soviet intelligence, the KGB. I loved my father very much, Paul. He was my entire world. I would do anything for him. Anything. So I willingly agreed to what became a life sentence.

For two years I helped Sophia gather information for the Russians about the Polish government in exile in London, and about Britain's many east European émigrés, especially those from the Baltic states. We mixed quite naturally with them because we too were refugees, and some confided that they worked for anti-Communist undergrounds in their homelands. I didn't ask how the Russians used this information. I didn't want to know.

They let me phone my father every few months. I didn't say what I was doing to help him. Our calls could just as well have been his reward for the specialised teaching the Russians needed for their nuclear program. We talked happily of places close to our hearts, the meadows, forests and cliffs of our wonderland by the Baltic Sea, and of our storytelling and funny little adventures and the chores and lessons we skipped to disappear for a while from the farm. We were full of hope. Each time we promised to see each other very soon.

After one of our calls, Sophia took me to a hotel near the Champs-Elysées and up to the mezzanine that overlooked the front entrance. We sat over coffee by the railing for a long time. She kept watching the door and I wondered what it was all about. Then you came in and she pointed you out. She said you were the information officer at the American embassy in London and a bachelor, and I was to make you my key to American and NATO affairs in Europe. Next day you were followed on your walk to the top of the Arc de Triomphe, and I was sent up to arrange our casual meeting with a question about that building on the distant hill. Remember, Paul?

I hated the thought of being a woman to any man, but you happened to be a wonderful companion and such a romantic. A few hours together and you were in love. I told you how Russian soldiers raped Mother and me and killed her to show my dread of Russia, something I never got over. You were a good source. You liked to be with me. You liked to talk about your work, even to criticise American policy and defence measures in Europe. But my Russian masters decided I could do better if I was closer to your official circles. They said I must marry you. I protested. They suggested my father might suffer if I didn't. I needed no further persuasion.

Our marriage did indeed profit the Russians. I shared your diplomatic privileges. I was welcomed among your colleagues and official contacts. I'm sure they saw me as another harmless and credulous embassy wife and mother. Many were naively charmed out of military and policy titbits. And you brought your work and gossip home.

You were a little jealous, I think, of a Swedish journalist and a French NATO officer. They were Russian agents. I was unfaithful only with Sophia. But you gave me Meg and Tim. Meg was myself as a child. Through her I relived those wonderful years with my father. I shall miss her very much on my journey. The idyllic years in our country retreat in England were ended all too soon by more Russian demands on me.

When the US entered the war against the Vietcong, the Soviet spy system in Southeast Asia was expanded to keep track of American and Seato moves. Sophia said I was to be part of it. Your embassy position had helped me do well in London so it was felt I could make good use of it in Vietnam. I was to convince you that a transfer to Saigon would be good for your career, but you had already thought of it and needed only my enthusiasm to apply. Sophia and I parted in tears the night before we flew from London.

But your Saigon post took you up-country quite often, and for long periods I produced nothing. Soon my contact, the manager of a European news bureau, urged me to find another embassy source to satisfy our masters. I snared an American aid official who bubbled over in bed with valuable information about US moves in Vietnam. When our affair became gossip I ended it, as he believed, for my family's sake. But his wife was now a good friend and I couldn't risk having her find out and perhaps creating a scene that might jeopardise the work which helped father survive.

It was the beginning of my drift from you, Paul. Forgive my cruelty. I now had to play the field as a carefree, sympathetic and available companion. It was productive, and it came to serve another purpose. Years ago, when I was truly married to you at last but still under Sophia's spell, I began to have strange and demanding cravings. They frightened me and I resisted, believing they sprang from that terrible rape. But in the voluptuous and sensual atmosphere of these tropics I gave in. I satisfied my cravings, and it brought peace, if just for a while.

That was my state when I became a Saigon wife in Bangkok. I soon cultivated good sources here and gathered the best in a circle of intimate friends. You met them on your visits to see the children. The men were especially helpful. Men like to tell what they know to loving, sympathetic women. My position as an American embassy wife put them even more at ease. It was almost a game.

Carl actually drew maps and took me on some flights to show how Unistates Air drops arms and supplies to anti-Communist hill tribes in Vietnam and Laos. My information helped North Vietnam capture some of the drops, but I was upset when they shot down one of the planes. I had met the crew and liked them. Carl was also my airbus to Vientiane where a Soviet agent, a French bartender, shared some assignments. My only contact in Bangkok was Lev, a press attaché at the Soviet embassy. He established an open, social relationship with our crowd by getting Betty to introduce him to my parties.

Dear Frank spared nothing on US Air Force strength and operations in Thailand, from bombing missions to helicopter searches for flyers lost over Vietnam and Laos. He also showed me around the B-52 base and American and Thai navy complex at Saddahip on the Gulf of Thailand, and the Russians were pleased with my description of its underground command and communications centre and storage for fuel and ammunition.

Freddy and Ward were my unsuspecting eyes and ears at Seato. They kept me posted on its war games, defence preparations and internal disputes, and how far the alliance might allow the communist Pathet Lao to advance in Laos before it considered intervention. But Seato must have worried that its secrets were getting out. A few weeks ago Ward told me its officials had been warned that Soviet

spies may be among their most intimate friends, and he joked that
since I was his most intimate friend I could be one of them. It gave
us a good laugh, but he'll never know how close he was to the truth.

Information from Jim, and my own observations on sales trips I
made with him, let Thai communist guerrillas know when and where
to make damaging attacks on American air bases in the North-East.
But Jim's most valuable contribution were advance cargo manifests on
ships bound for Bangkok. He wormed them out of his loving Maria
when I suggested they might be useful to black market friends who
could be helpful to his business. In fact the manifests also detected
the arrival of American military supplies, and a great deal went over
ship sides into the speedboats of Thai insurgents.

I took advantage of Wilma's confidential gossip from friends in the
CIA and the American embassy, Susan's knowledge of Jusmag and
the training of Thai special forces, and Betty's role as confidante of
high society and its military and government connections. I even had
help of sorts from that church couple, Ralph and Beatrice. They
stayed with my children when my work took me out of town, though
it led to a strange and violent episode that few people would
understand and I won't try to explain.

Jill needs no explanation. Our relationship was obvious. She
fulfilled a craving that Sophia awakened in me years ago. Of all those
close to me in Bangkok only Jill escaped the way I used people in my
work for Soviet intelligence. I lost all conscience. I convinced
myself that what I did had little bearing on events of any importance.
I did it only for Father's sake.

My last phone call to him was from the Soviet embassy in Tokyo
when I went there last year for cosmetic surgery on my breasts. He
sounded old and tired, longing to be back home by the Baltic Sea. We
said nothing of our dream of being together again one day. Perhaps
he now wondered as I did if our Russian masters felt such dreams
were sufficient in themselves, and they didn't necessarily have to let
them come true. At least they were letting us exchange letters every
few months by way of diplomatic pouches and Lev, my Bangkok
contact. I filled my letters with stories about his grandchildren and
their pictures. He thought of us as a happy family, and he wrote of
our own wonderfully tender years before the nightmare of war.

And now, dear Paul, I come to the end of my tale. Not long ago I
was confronted with evidence of one of my attempts to get American

military information. It was conclusive, and much of my work over the years seemed to be known as well. It's a mystery how an American embassy wife came to be suspected of being a Soviet spy, but someone I trusted was used to trap me. It would be futile to name my betrayer or the agency they acted for, and I've made sure this letter shields everyone from suspicion.

I was given time to decide if I would buy my freedom with all I knew of Soviet espionage in Southeast Asia, or face arrest, trial and prison, and the shame it would bring to my family. I thought of escape. I didn't tell my Russian masters I had been found out. I begged Lev to persuade them to let me and my children join my father in Moscow as a reward for all my success as a spy. It was then that he told me, finally and reluctantly, that a heart attack had killed my father soon after his last letter two months before.

I felt myself wither, Paul. My life seemed to bleed away. I was an empty shell of pain. I had not seen my father for nearly twenty-five years, yet he was always close, always a part of me. I never stopped believing we would be together again in this life. Lev could see my hurt. He said I had no reason to go to Moscow now, and I wouldn't be allowed to quit because my work was valuable. He advised me to carry on for my own safety's sake.

Now I felt very alone, so weary, confused and unprotected. For days I agonised over my father's death and my discovery, trying to keep up my pretence of carefree detachment, and savouring my pleasures as though each was the last.

Tonight my betrayer brought a final notice. I had only two more days to choose a course. As they tried again to persuade me to turn informer, I began to realise that I have known all along the path I want to take.

I am going to my father. I know where he is, and I know the way. Tell my dear sweet Meg we shall wait for her there. She will understand. Take good care of her, Paul. Meg needs your love. And little Tim wants his daddy. You'll enjoy him, I know. I love my children very much, but it's better that they see no more of me as I have become. They will be fine in your kind hands. Thank you, dear Paul, for your love and our time of happiness. Forgive me for the pain I brought you.

Madli

Chapter Eighteen

Rising slowly to his feet, and tucking Madli's little pistol into a back pocket of his khaki drills, Somsak stepped nimbly to the screen door where he had left his shoes when he came in from the garden with Susan many hours before. He picked them up, tiptoed to the front door, and slipped them on. Then, retrieving his uniform cap from a clothes hook under the stairs, he faced the silent room.

Hands thrust in his pockets, Ward paced up and down by the wall of screened windows, his gaze distant and melancholy; from her cushion by the table, Betty watched, her warm brown eyes bright with feeling. On the sofa, Susan and Maria sat close, hands clasped and eyes shut as though in repose. Beside them, absently chewing gum and rolling an empty glass between his palms, Frank stared at the broad back of Carl; he slouched over the buffet, a bottle in his big fist, a sardonic grin on his beefy face.

Frozen astride her chair, Jill unconsciously clawed its back, her eyes riveted on Madli's letter as Paul, his face creased by fatigue, read it deliberately and to himself, his dry lips forming the painful words; on her cushion beside him, Meg rested her cheek on his knee, her slender body wilted, her eyes closed and shadowed.

Squeezing his cap under an arm, Somsak *wai*-ed a solemn farewell to Wilma; it was of no use; she clutched the arms of her chair, her eyes wide and unseeing. No one seemed aware that he was leaving. He opened the door, stepped outside, and closed it softly behind him.

The early morning air smelt fresh and clean. He breathed deeply, squinting at the rising sun's brilliant reflection in the top windows of the tall apartment block next door. He found the iron gate open and Alun there in yellow sarong and short white blouse, her waist-length hair brushed shiny black and her eyes sleepy. By her bare feet was a large pan of cold cooked rice, and she waited to scoop a dollop into the begging bowls of the monks who came each dawn for the gift of food that Buddhists believe earns merit in the donor's afterlife.

She *wai*-ed and smiled broadly. "*Sawadee*, Captain Somsak. *Dee mahg?*"

He returned her *wai* and patted the pistol in his back pocket. "*Dee mahg* - very good, Alun. *Sawadee.*"

He walked to his Lambretta, parked behind Jill's silver Porsche, and wedged his cap under its pillion strap. Unlocking the scooter, he began pushing it towards Sukhumvit Road, a long block away.

A few gates further on, two young monks emerged from a compound, skulls, eyebrows and jowls freshly shaved, furled black umbrellas hooked over their forearms, and black metal begging bowls peeping from within their long and loose orange robes. Somsak halted, rested the scooter against a leg, *wai*-ed reverently, and was rewarded with toothy grins.

At Sukhumvit, he backed the scooter onto its stand, lit a cigarette, inhaled deeply, and let the smoke escape lazily on his breath. He watched an early bus with a few drowsy passengers roar by on the wide main road, its boy conductor leaning carelessly out the rear door on one foot, its exhaust belching clouds of acrid diesel smoke into the still air; and for a while his attention settled aimlessly on a *sahmlaw* driver tinkering with his three-wheel taxi by the opposite curb.

He looked down Wilma's *soi*. Lush flame trees thrust bright yellow and scarlet blooms over high brick or stone walls here and there; and towering palms within the secluded compounds rose like skeletal sentinels against the cloudless sky. The young monks were far along the *soi* now, their robes flapping around bony ankles and dusty bare feet. He was on his third cigarette when a slight figure in pale blue came out of Wilma's gate and proceeded briskly towards Sukhumvit. He nodded and waited with expectation, smiling easily as she approached.

"I thought you'd be home by now," said Susan, returning his smile as she brushed her unruly blonde strand back in place once more.

He held up the cigarette. "My last before I go."

She checked her watch. "It's quite early. Will your family be up?"

"It's Sunday, there's no school, so the children will be awake before their usual time. And very noisy."

She laughed. "That sounds familiar. My father threatened us kids with his belt every Sunday morning but it didn't help. He seldom managed to sleep in."

"Sunday is one of many customs we borrowed from you. Surnames is another, for example. We adopted them when we got a postal service early in this century. They made it easier to deliver mail."

"But you still address everyone by first names. I like that."

"Last night you mentioned many things that you like about my country."

"I didn't mention this time of day," she said softly. "Its restful stillness, the fresh scents of flowers, unhurried monks on our *sois* and sleepy servants at our gates with traditional gifts of rice, small boys in tiny *sampans* plucking the heart of the lotus in the *klongs* in our gardens and beside the roads, the sounds of waking babies, puppies, birds, monkeys and geese, of kitchens and laundries coming to life..."

"Yet our tranquil mornings always herald another scorcher," he said, looking towards an ominous red ball of sun over the far rooftops.

"Yes, and after early mass at Holy Redeemer, and a leisurely breakfast in the Erawan tearoom, I shall spend most of this one in the pool at the Thai officers' club."

"And our friends back there...?"

"Probably a raid on the GI's Villa Club for loads of beer so they can drink the day away under beach umbrellas on Wilma's lawn."

He grinned. "I can imagine. And when you left...?"

"Well," she sighed, gazing down the *soi*, "Noi, Dang and little Tim still slept. Ward and Betty nestled on the sofa, looking thoughtful yet somehow content. Frank and Carl showered noisily upstairs, and Maria and Alun tidied up and chattered away in Thai. I could hear Freddy slurring through 'Waltzing Matilda' in Wilma's bedroom so I guess he's well into that bottle of gin. And in the garden..."

A pensive pause, then quietly: "Meg and her father were by the *klong*. They held hands and seemed to have a certain peace. Wilma was there, explaining how the lotus cycle opens the soft white flower at night and closes it at dawn. That's how they were when I left... But wait. There's Jill. Paul had let her hold Madli's letter, and she was reading it yet again."

"Surely the letter was discussed...?"

She shook her head. "Not even mentioned, though I rather think they'll face up to it when they're at ease over drinks again. I think they'll keep it quiet. Really. It's too painful, too embarrassing."

"And there's no telling if Miss Meg would have produced the pistol and letter eventually, or left her mother's mysterious last visitor under suspicion of murder. A good thing they were discovered by chance in Tim's school bag."

She winced. "Dear Meg. The distressing thoughts and scenes that must haunt her. I hope Paul takes her away from Southeast Asia. She's known too much sorrow here."

"Her mother's an obsession."

"As Madli's father was to her. Love and devotion make people do extraordinary things, don't they? In helping him survive in Russia she caused heartache, treason, and probably deaths. Some would find it hard to understand."

"They might find it hard to understand what you did as well, Miss Susan."

"What *I* did...?" she queried, taken by surprise.

"Yes. What you did for the agency that suspected Mrs. Madli was a Soviet spy."

"*Agency*...? Good heavens, Somsak. What are you getting at...?"

He smiled. "I think you know."

"I'm afraid I don't," she replied simply.

"Miss Susan, from all I observed back there, only you could have set the trap that snared Mrs. Madli."

"Somsak... !"

"One moment. You said Mrs. Madli suggested that you take her spare room while you both groomed Sumalee for a Jusmag job. Miss Betty says Mrs. Madli complained that you almost foisted yourself and the girl on her. Mrs. Wilma said Mrs. Madli seemed upset about something when she told her she had asked you to leave. Had you confronted her with the evidence you gathered with the help of a make-believe bar girl? A more likely reason than your words over Mrs. Madli's behaviour. You kept your key. I think you used it on the night she -"

"Come on, Somsak," she cut in lightly. "You can't be serious."

"You haven't denied it," he persisted. "And you know you can trust me."

"That's not the point..." Yet slowly, as if resigned, she allowed herself a little smile. "Of course I can. Just as you trusted me with information last night." He grinned his appreciation, and she took a deep breath. "Well, Somsak, I suppose our friends think the CIA tripped Madli up. In fact it was Thai Intelligence. Since Americans here are known to hold secrets like a sieve, the CIA was kept in the dark. But Madli's nemesis was that Polish trade attaché..."

"Ah. Some back there believe corrupt customs officers killed him for cheating on their crooked deals, then bribed police to say he was killed in a robbery by a Chinese seaman who has simply vanished."

"That word came from a higher authority, you said. I think it was a ruse to throw nosy reporters off the scent. Apparently the Pole was murdered at Klong Toey by Soviet Intelligence, the KGB. He worked for them. They silenced him when they discovered he was trying to defect to the West with Thailand's help. But they weren't aware that when he asked for refuge he sweetened the pill by telling Thai Intelligence a little of what he knew of Soviet espionage in Southeast Asia. He refused to give names until he was accepted, but he left a hint that among the KGB spies was one of Bangkok's several Saigon wives with American embassy connections..."

"Hard to believe, I would think."

"It was. But they investigated the lot. Eventually their suspicions centred on Madli because of her origins, her odd activities in Vietnam, Thailand and Laos, and her intimacy with insiders like Ward, Freddy, Frank, Carl, Jim, Wilma's Dick, and her own husband. It seemed to tie in with certain successes by Soviet protégés, the Vietcong, Pathet Lao and Thai and Malaysian insurgents. And with an underground circulation of classified information about American and Seato plans, policies and military bases. There was no evidence of Madli's hand, so they cooked up a scheme that only a foreigner familiar to Madli's crowd could pull off."

"And they chose you. Why...?"

She smiled shyly. "Because I look harmless enough to fool anybody, I guess. I'm trusted. Jusmag checked me out before I could teach English to the officers they pick for special training in the States. And the academy knows I'm fond of your country, and worried about the danger it's in from the wars next door. In asking me, Thai Intelligence filled me in on everything, including the damage and deaths blamed on spies. Strange, really. They seemed to appeal to patriotism. In the end I was persuaded by feelings. I've told you, haven't I, of the peace, purpose and home I found here? I could do something in return..."

"A rare gratitude from a foreigner, Miss Susan. They must be pleased with you."

"And with Sumalee. She's a well-educated daughter of an army general in the North-West, and was quite convincing in the role of a simple bar girl. It took little foisting to hook Madli. She saw the advantages of having a devoted ally in Jusmag. Sumalee assured her of that. She swore she'd do anything in the world to repay Madli's kindness if she got the job. Once she was there, Madli soon made use of her. She got Sumalee to make copies of classified documents, claiming they were needed by the American embassy to make a secret check on US military advisers. Sumalee brought fake papers, naturally. She also made several indiscreet and incriminating phone calls to her that were taped. I had to confront Madli with the evidence..."

She sighed, shaking her head at the thought. "It was very hard to do. I'd become fond of her and the children. I felt like a Judas. She was terribly distressed. She couldn't believe I could do this to her. She said I'd understand why she spied for the Russians if I knew her reasons, though she wouldn't give them. I begged her, for the sake of her family, to choose freedom in exchange for all she knew of Soviet espionage. But she carried on as though she could brazen her way through. Her letter tells how she learned of her father's death. The Russians had cruelly kept them apart and made her pay for his life. But they couldn't stop her joining him now. So she did. It was what she wanted." She looked at him enquiringly. "Somsak, how will you solve her death?"

"Well, the newspapers have decided that Mrs. Madli was murdered by a *kamoy*. Next week we can agree. Some day police will kill a *kamoy* in one of those gunfights that happen now and then. We'll say he had the pistol that took her life and blame him for the crime. I think that higher authority will approve. But what crossed your mind when you heard of her death and its circumstances?"

"I wondered if the KGB had learned that she had been found out, and after I left had silenced her as they did the Polish trade attaché. When we were told who had keys to her house, I wondered if one of the others was a Soviet agent and had let in her killer." She shuddered. "What a shameful suspicion to have of one's friends."

"But as you say, they probably suspect the CIA tripped her up."

She nodded. "And since many *farangs* think every other *farang* is in the CIA's pay, I'm sure they'd rather not know the identity of Madli's last visitor. It's all too close for comfort. When they're in their cups somebody's role in Madli's dangerous game might be recalled to amuse, or to wound. That could happen today if it's Carl, with his clumsy humour, who tells Freddy and Jim about her letter."

"It also cleared up the mystery of Ward's suspicions," he reminded her. "She said Ward had told her of a Seato warning that Soviet spies could be in Bangkok's most intimate circles. And last night's rambling revelations made him see at last how she might have used him and the others."

"Quite shattering to some, I imagine. But I don't think it will tarnish Ward's loving memories of her."

"Ah. You found a pleasant thought in all this. But you must be surprised that Miss Meg allowed her mother's letter to be read...?"

"Not really, Somsak. It completes her punishment of those she blames the most for her mother's destruction."

"Poor child," he murmured. "Only a great deal of tender care can set her mind at rest. Still, I'm glad Mrs. Madli realised the futility of naming her last visitor. You're in the clear, Miss Susan."

Her eyes clouded. "Far from it, Somsak," she said sadly. "It was I who betrayed Madli and caused Meg's great loss. I must live with that guilt."

"Now see here, Miss Susan," he protested. "You mustn't..." His eye caught a movement down the *soi*. "Look. Someone in black leaves Mrs. Wilma's compound."

She turned, her face softening. "Maria. Such a graceful walk. She too needs tender care after last night."

"Miss Susan," he said, suddenly purposeful. "Our house in Lumpini police compound is third on the right. A few pots of orchids hang below, a little bougainvillaea struggles up the concrete stilts, and the laundry line is heavy with children's clothes. It's a family home of spirited youngsters and easy parents."

Pushing the Lambretta off its stand, he swung a leg over the saddle, kicked the starter, revved the motor a little, and faced her, serious now. "You are always welcome."

She touched his arm, smiling faintly. "*Sawadee*, Somsak."

"*Sawadee*, Miss Susan."

He returned her *wai*, put the scooter in gear with a touch of his toe on the pedal, accelerated along the left curb, and turned right into the increasing traffic on Sukhumvit. A short block and he stopped for a red light at Soi Nana. He looked back down the sidewalk. Susan and Maria walked hand in hand towards Ruam Rudee and the Church of The Holy Redeemer.

The light changed. He gunned the scooter two quick blocks, bumped over the railway crossing, and eased it into the inside traffic lane. Two more blocks and he turned left at Wireless Road, and into the cool shade of the huge trees that meet over the street and its roadside *klongs* for the full half mile to Lumpini.

The End